Must Love Jelly Beans

by

Ginny Frost

Copyright

Must Love Jelly Beans

Contact Information: **ginnyfrost@ginnyfrost.com**

Ginny Frost
PO Box 4686
Halfmoon, NY 12065-9211

Visit me at **www.ginnyfrost.com**

Published in the United States of America

Edited by **ColeHearted Editing**

Cover Image via depositphotos.com by Betka82

Also by Ginny Frost

The Oakwood Tavern Series
- The Bar Scene
- Swindled
- Stranded
- When Hearts Collide

Stonewater Stories
- The Carriage House
- Christmas Sparks
- Christmas Affair
- Christmas Baby
- New Year's Miracle

Artist

Dedication

For the Barnes Crew—I never would have finished the book without you.

Acknowledgments

I would like to thank Tib and Brian for helping me get through this book. You both kept me working and moving forward, even when I didn't wan to.

A huge thank you to Kari for editing my mess and turning it into a pretty good book. I'm eternally grateful for your time and effort, my friend.

And my lovely coworkers, who asked on a monthly basis "When is the jelly bean book coming out?" Love you all.

Chapter One

Holly Lincoln glanced around the garish shop. Color assaulted her from every angle. McIntyre's Sweets, a local candy shop buried in northern New York, was the last place she wanted to be. Somewhere on the planet, combatants waged war, but here she stood, journalism degree in hand, talking to a local candy guy about his beans.

Jelly beans.

Someone shoot me.

She'd driven three hours north to talk to a grown man about jelly beans. Instead of standing in a war-torn countryside, interviewing refugees, she waited in the middle of a mom-and-pop shop. With a shake of her head, she scanned the walls and shelves again. Since she merited an actual paying gig, it might be best to jot notes about the place.

The shelves held nothing but pure sugar as far as the eye could see. One wall was lined with colorful bags and small boxes in every color of the rainbow. On the other side, a glass case showcased jelly beans by the thousands. Five hundred different flavors filled the little bins. Lacy paper stuck out from each tray, cradling the candy like a baby.

Its old-world vibe sang with the dark oak shelves and counter. But the rainbow color scheme said teenage girl with a credit card. It resembled every small-town shop in the Northeast, if those shops were high on marshmallows.

Holly sighed. Her low-sugar diet did not help in completing the assignment. Not to mention, her beloved gray-on-gray suit made her stick out like a sore thumb. She glanced down at her mauve shoes, her one concession to wearing color. She hated color on her, on her skin, in her hair, and here she was surrounded by every hue in the universe.

Why did her boss always send her these stupid stories? Jelly beans? Really? Who even liked jelly beans?

"Can I help you, miss?" A low baritone sounded behind her.

Holly snapped out of her internal rant. She spun, putting on her best cub reporter's face.

"Hi." Her grin froze on her lips.

A hunky male with flaming red hair smiled at her from behind the counter. His cornflower-blue eyes blazed out of freckled skin. His shoulders spanned across the room, and his chiseled chin caused her mouth to water. He looked oversized and out of place in the unicorn explosion of a store. How did a vision of the perfect romance icon Scot end up in a candy store?

He raised one red eyebrow. "Hi?"

Holly blinked several times, shoving images of kilts, cabers, and bearded men out of her head. "Hi, I'm looking for Mr. McIntyre. I'm Holly Lincoln from Adirondack Chronicles Magazine."

The Adonis grinned. "Hey! I'm Callum McIntyre."

Holly's jaw dropped, and she kicked herself for bailing on researching the piece. Spring in northern New

York had her dreaming of fields of flowers and lush new green leaves. The assignment boiled down to three days in the woods with the hillbillies. She figured she could do research during the long, boring nights in the tiny town.

No one told her the owner was not an old man, rotund on sweets, but a hunky Scot with eyelashes for days.

She flashed a weak smile and waggled her fingers.

With grace no one his size should have, he moved across the floor to an opening in the counter and slid through. Towering over her at six feet plus, he held out his hand. "I'm glad to meet you, Holly. Welcome to my shop." He grasped her hand and pumped it up and down.

Holly melted a little. "This is *your* shop?" she asked, worried she'd screwed up the gig already.

He released her grip and put his fists on his hips.

Holly's brain flashed to every Scottish romance book cover ever. *Oh my God, someone get the man a plaid shirt and a large wood ax.*

"Yeah, I'm still working on the redecorating. I want the store to feel fun and impulsive, but I may have gone a skitch too far." He rubbed his chin. "Anyway, sorry for making you wait."

What? Did he mean the two seconds she'd stood in the store? Okay. The man emitted serious vibes, but Holly felt unsure what it all meant. The truth of the situation eluded her.

"Uh, it's fine. I wanted to check out the place. It appears…" She glanced around, not wanting to hurt the man's feelings.

"Too garish, too loud…?" He rolled his wrist at the wall of shelves.

"Too teenage girl's bedroom?" she supplied and slapped her hand over her mouth. *Okay, it was a shit assignment, but not Callum's fault*. She shouldn't insult his livelihood.

Instead of a glare or a grimace, he laughed. "How did you know my neighbor's niece helped me? Yeah, she's ten, and well, I've been focused on cooking." He shrugged. "We'll muddle through."

"Cooking?" she asked and pressed her lips to stop betraying her ignorance. She should have known. Way to show her lack of research. Her cheeks blazed hot, and she turned her head to hide her embarrassment.

"Yeah. Wanna see my kitchen?" His huge grin

infected her, and she grinned back. He grabbed her hand, dragged her behind the counter, and through a large oak door in the rear of the shop.

What had she gotten into?

Cal marveled at his renovated kitchen. His gran ran the store for decades, but now he stood at the helm. Unless she showed up, which she did when she felt compelled to create candy. So, once a week.

Already, a huge, well, medium-sized magazine sent an actual reporter to his store for a story. He'd get press, and new customers, and old customers, and more. He bit his lip to contain a scream of joy.

He glanced at the reporter, and his brain zeroed in on her color scheme. She looked gray, not old-person gray or a shabby gray, but dressed in various shades of the color from head to toe.

Huh.

And he still held her arm.

He released her. His wild energy always landed him in trouble.

She blinked at him with a small smile. New people always responded that way. He didn't care. She'd either get used to him or not.

"So"—he flung his arms wide—"this is where the magic happens." He did a slow circle, pointing to mixers, supply shelves, ovens, and racks.

Her expression never changed from the weird smile. "Magic beans?" she asked.

"Yes!" He jumped toward her, grabbing both her hands. "Yes, they are totally magic. Homemade, handmade, fresh as fresh can be. And once you taste them…" He released her hands and threw his arms out in an explosive gesture. "You'll be hooked!"

He spun around the room, showing her his marvelous kitchen, his mouth blabbering on at a hundred miles an hour. It took him a few minutes before he calmed down, remembering she planned to interview him. She was not an old friend touring his new kitchen.

He pressed his lips together and caught the reporter's eye. Well, more like her wide-eyed, open-mouthed gape.

"I was rambling, huh?" he asked, allowing some serious sheepishness to enter his tone. He forgot that sometimes not everyone was his new best friend or as enthusiastic about his job as he was. He pulled in a breath and repeated in his head, *Not everyone is as into this as you are.*

When he remained quiet for a minute, her cold expression melted.

"Well, you sure are passionate about your business," she said, her words a shade away from icy. "Can we slow things down? I don't have my recorder out yet. I can't take notes as fast as you speak." Her smile looked fake.

He'd lost her in two minutes.

A new record.

Cal held up his hands. "Okay, sorry. I tend to go on." He met her skeptical gaze. "No, it's not the sugar." He tried to sober up, but the thrill of being featured in a magazine article threw his brain into fireworks.

"Alright." She raised an eyebrow and gestured to the work counter. "Can we sit? And get comfortable. Let's talk basics first. I know nothing about candy making."

"Oh, of course." He waved her over to the metal stools. Ahead of himself again and always.

She slid into a seat, all smooth steel and grace.

Cal gulped a breath. He'd failed to take a good look at the woman except for her color choice. He paused for a second to drink her in.

The reporter sat in the chair as if she belonged there. Her shapely legs crossed under her gray skirt, giving an air of supreme elegance. Her back stood board-straight with her black braid centered perfectly. Her hands lay folded on the counter, her long fingers the epitome of elegance.

His breath caught in his throat. They sent a smart, sophisticated woman. *Fantastic*. She'd dismiss him in a second if she hadn't already.

He slid into a seat across from her and drew his lips into a tight smile. "Okay, yes." He folded his hands the same as hers. "I'm Callum McIntyre, and this is my candy shop."

She smiled, and his heart pinged. He might be in trouble here. Beautiful women caused his ADHD to launch into overdrive. He'd be tongue-tied and tripping over his own feet.

"Yes, I know." She pulled out a digital recorder and a small laptop. "I have a few topics I want to cover.

You've spoken with my editor. He wants a three-part series on the shop as a feature piece in our local color section. I generated a small outline, but it will be better with your input on what to highlight."

He stared at her blankly. She was the writer. Why ask him? What did he want to feature? Everything but that sounded like too much. She could highlight his new items or do the history of the store. Should he bring Gran here? He should call her.

He stood, and she grasped his hand. "Hold on there."

A shock of electricity ran up his arm. He stopped halfway out of his chair. He plopped into his seat, his mouth gaping open.

"Where are you going?" She pulled her hand away, brow furrowed.

"Sorry. My brain has a mind of its own." He smiled. "Whatever you want or need to do is good. I make candy. I'm not a writer."

She studied him for a second before saying, "Fine." Her tone held a hint of annoyance. "I want it to play out like this." She spun her laptop to face him.

A dozen apps appeared to be open, crowding the screen. A detailed outline covered the center, but his eyes crossed trying to read the text. Cal ran his fingers through his red hair, lifting it into spikes.

"Uh," he said, bending over the machine. "Looks as if you've already done the work." He met her eye and winked. "You don't even need me."

For some bizarre reason, the woman's face flushed like a house on fire, and she seemed lost for words.

"I'm sorry." She fluttered before taking a breath and beginning again. As quickly as the first change, she became the calm, cool reporter again. "I filled in the pertinent information. But it won't replace the personal touch your answers bring. The outline is a guide for our conversations."

Cal gazed at her, his head cocked to the side like Tess's cocker spaniel puppy. His mind wandered to the topic of dogs. *Gus is such a good pup*. His focus returned to the crowded laptop. He pressed the power button and closed the lid.

"Let's forget it for now and chat. I might not talk your ear off about most subjects." He held up a finger. "*But*... When it comes to candy, I'm an encyclopedia." He winked again, and her color flushed to a darker shade of pink.

Cool, she felt as flustered as he did. He could work with that.

Holly pursed her lips and glanced at her closed laptop. The next three days might prove interesting, albeit exhausting, with this one. “Tell me about the store,” she prompted.

He slapped his hand on the counter and launched from his stool, which clanged to the ground. He zoomed around the table and pulled her to her feet. “We’ll start with a tour.” He grabbed her hand and headed out of the kitchen into the showroom.

Holly suppressed a laugh as the man glanced around the store as if he’d never been in his own candy shop before.

“Well,” he said, taking a deep breath. “There it is.” He held his arms out as if that answered everything.

Holly would have to pull the information out of him or have his staff show her the details of the store. The place was supposed to be the center of the article. With her first impression of Cal, she decided to place him as the focal point of the story. Then she could run the fluff about the shop around his odd, hyper personality. And if he was as good a confectioner as her boss boasted…

"Do you run the entire shop, or do you have assistants?"

Cal scratched his head. "Suzanne's my manager, and Wendy helps with cooking and sales. They're around here somewhere… I create all the candy. Wanna make some?" He tugged at her arm, pulling her toward the kitchen again.

Holly balked. The interview was running around in circles. "Tell me about the items you sell. Please be specific. It will give the article depth. I want mouths watering over your creations. I can't say, 'There it is,' and show a grainy picture." She lowered her head and glared at him properly. "Show me the candy."

He cocked his head and stared deep into her eyes.

A flush of heat rolled over her to have someone contemplate her with such depth. She pulled away, and the movement broke the spell.

"Yes," he said with a little jump in the air. "Let me show you the candy. We've recently rearranged several items. Please be patient with me if I can't find stuff. Suzanne talked about customer flow, where they pause, or where they need to consider choices, and not just grab. Anyway, she has this system. I have no idea what it is, but I know what's in each case."

"Well, that's good." Holly suppressed another laugh. The guy certainly got rolling with his little speeches. She found his manor endearing and a little intimidating. Of course, he knew the inventory. Didn't he make everything?

She frowned. The story was supposed to be about a great candy maker, hidden in the upper Adirondacks. What if he'd bought everything at Walmart and resold it? What if the place ended up being nothing more than a mall candy store?

"Confession time." He nudged her with his elbow. "I don't make everything."

Holly's shoulders fell as her worst nightmare came to life. No cute custom-made candy, no award-winning humanity piece. No promotion. No hope of getting out of the Living section.

"Everyone helps—Suzanne, Wendy, Grandma. Not Grandma as much as before. But everyone pitches in. I create recipes and do most of the heavy work. Wendy is a master decorator. Check out these brittles."

He grabbed her hand and pulled her over to one of the glass cases.

"We bake brittle everything—cashew, pecan, peanut." He tapped on the glass. "But Wendy will decorate them like cookies. She picks a theme and goes nuts." He laughed at his own pun.

Holly glanced into the case. Various types of brittle candy filled the six shelves, but in the middle, one tray held twelve elaborately decorated egg-shaped pieces. Each one resembled a Faberge egg, gold lacing and all.

"They're gorgeous," she stuttered. The story might work after all.

"Yeah." Cal touched the glass as if petting the eggs. "She's great at it. She's into embroidery and said, 'Why don't we create threads on them?' I didn't want cotton on my candy, except for the cotton candy, which I do in summer. But she meant frosting. And boom, we had a new product." He grinned.

Holly got lost in his words and the decorations on the candy.

"So, is it okay if it's a team effort? I don't want to

lie to you about anything. We work together. Grandma creates the homemade marshmallows. Well, most of it. She loves using her cookie cutters. Wendy decorates those, too."

He dragged her over to a case. Inside, one shelf contained tons of little animals, flowers, and shapes, decorated with frosting.

"These are homemade marshmallows?"

"Yeah, they take for-ev-er to set. So, Grandma always volunteers to make them. She brings over her cutters and mixes everything here. Completely health code compliant. She can't do it at home and bring them in. Though she forgets sometimes." He shrugged.

He grasped Holly's hand again and pulled her to yet another case. "Over here are the mixed nut combos, big with the hikers. The obligatory fudge counter. You can't have a tourist shop in New York without fudge. And the wall of gummies. We've got everything you could want in a gummy. The grown-up versions are in the back."

Holly raised an eyebrow.

Red tinged his cheeks. "No, not like that. The ones with wine or booze in them. I can't sell them to the kids. Yes, I have a license to sell them. Adults have to ask. I put the flavors on the chalkboard with names the kiddos won't know about or care about."

His energy appeared boundless. He pulled her along to a fourth glass case. "And the jelly beans. Again, the 'over twenty-one' ones are in the back. We have every flavor. And I mean every one!" He waved his hand at the wild colors and various-sized jelly beans.

Holly marveled at the sheer number of them. Something niggled at the back of her brain. She glanced around the room, her brain ticking. With Cal silenced for a second, her own brain started working again.

"Cal," she said with the tone of a horror movie heroine. "There's no chocolate."

Chapter Two

"Can we do an off-the-record thing?"

Holly put her pen down, though she sensed he'd tell her something with real teeth for her story. She'd never betray such a nice man if he didn't want his story told. Inside, she quivered at the idea she'd asked the right question—the moment when you hit on the one question that caused people to spill their guts, priceless.

Cal stared at the shelves for a few more seconds, and she waited until his thoughts reconciled. His expression grew dower, and shadows darkened his eyes.

The mention of chocolate certainly stirred something up.

He closed his eyelids for a beat, then met her gaze dead on. "We'll keep that topic for another time. I'd rather show you what we do have."

Holly kept her breathing slow. *Not an earth-shattering secret, but definitely something.* She'd have to get him talking again later.

"We need pizza."

"Pizza?" she asked, scratching her head as he towed her toward the back door.

"Best in town. I'm going to lunch," he called over his shoulder to no one as he escorted Holly out the door into the alley.

"But you didn't answer my question."

"Lunch first," he said and grasped her hand. The thrill of contact sparked again. "Hey, what's your name, anyway?"

"Holly?" It sounded more like a question than a statement as she stumbled behind him in her tall, mauve heels. "Wait, I already told you my name."

"You sure about that?" He winked.

What the hell have I gotten myself into?

Holly stumbled behind Cal as he guided her into an alley and onto the main street. Her shoes were not built for the graveled terrain nor the fast pace the man insisted upon.

Nothing inside her warned her to stop or wait or call him out for his pushy behavior. Usually, she'd never allowed men to order her around. Well, except for her father.

But Cal, he seemed to be a force of nature. And when he paused to consider something, she could practically see his merry-go-round brain spinning.

He paused at the sidewalk, glancing both ways before crossing the road.

Holly took advantage of the moment and stopped him. "One second, please."

He spun to face her, seemed to realize he held her hand, and released it. But not before giving her a warm squeeze. The little gesture sent tingles up and down her arm. *What the hell was happening here?* She required a minute to process.

One second, they stood in the shop, and the next, in the kitchen. Now they were in the street, running somewhere.

"If you don't like pizza, they have other choices."

Holly raised her hands. She'd dealt with difficult

men her entire life. Men who told her what to do, men who underestimated her, men who assumed she was useless because she was a woman. She lacked patience for such behavior.

"Look. I need to interview you. Can we sit in the shop and have a conversation, rather than running through the street?" The words came out harsher than she'd meant, but the entire encounter left her head spinning.

Cal's bottom lip puckered out, and his gaze dropped to his shoes. "Sorry. I get ahead of myself sometimes." He shuffled his feet, resembling every reprimanded little boy on the planet. "I thought we'd talk over lunch."

Holly sighed. How could she be angry at such an enthusiastic guy? He wasn't trying to be annoying or controlling. He just didn't seem to have a filter.

"Sure. We can have lunch. But ask me next time before hauling me into the street. I mean, look at my shoes."

Cal glanced at her shoes. "Those are completely impractical for walking around Bakersville. But sexy as hell."

Their gazes met, and heat rushed to her face again. She always blushed easily and worked hard to keep the red from her face. Something about Cal threw her off her game and made her flush like a schoolgirl. At least, he looked similarly embarrassed.

He scrubbed the back of his neck. “Sorry. I tend to think in confusing blurts. Anyway…” He took a deep breath as the color receded from his face. “Do you want to go to the shop or eat lunch?”

Much to Holly’s further embarrassment, her stomach growled with gusto.

He laughed. Not a chuckle over the embarrassing situation, but a full-on belly laugh. And her face reddened with heat again.

“Lunch then,” he stated once he calmed down. “I’m sorry. I’m not laughing at you, but at your perfect comedic timing.” He held out an elbow. “Come on. My treat. I promise not to drag you anywhere else.”

A little shiver ran over Holly as she hooked her arm in his. *He won’t be dragging me again? That’s a damn shame.*

They strolled across the street into a busy pizza parlor straight out of every small-town TV show. She glanced around at the checkered tablecloths, olive-skinned, dark-haired waitstaff bustling here and there. They called out with accents from both New York City and the Mediterranean.

But the scent of tomato sauce and garlic caused Holly to fall in love at first smell.

Cal waved to a few staffers and sat in an empty booth. He'd marched right past the "Wait to Be Seated" sign.

Holly stalled next to it, hating to break the rules. Cal waved her over, but she pointed at the sign. A young man with dark hair and dancing black eyes stopped at the hostess station and winked at her. Now, two men in the town had winked at her. *What was with Bakersville*?

"Cal always seats himself." The man shrugged. "We let him in because he's good for business." The waiter waved her over to Cal's table. "Any friend of his…" His voice sounded low and sexy, something that normally would've induced either a warning sign or goosebumps.

Neither happened.

Now, when she noticed Cal's shining smile and eager expression, those goosebumps arrived in droves.

She did not know what was happening, but she feigned indifference and sat across from him anyway.

"What do you like?" he asked, thrusting a menu at her. The question felt intimate.

In her twenty-seven years of living in upstate New York, she'd never met a pizza she enjoyed. They either tasted too sweet, were too thin, or had weird spices. And since it was lunch, she shouldn't order a giant plate of spaghetti and meatballs.

So, then, pizza…

"Cheese is fine." She perused the menu anyway, which displayed every Italian dish on the planet on its two oversized pages. Gawking at the listings, she pulled in a breath and closed the menu.

"You could eat here every night and never have the same meal twice in a month." Cal grinned as a young brunette stopped at their table. She appeared bored and tired, her hair limp, her black T-shirt dusted with flour.

"Same, Cal?" she asked, and met Holly's gaze. The kohl around her eyes cracked as she stared at Holly. "Who the hell is this?" She thrust out a hip and crossed her arms.

Holly examined the woman. She looked young for Cal, but she might be his girlfriend. Again, Holly regretted not doing more research on the man, the town, and the candy shop.

"Nadia, meet Holly. She's a reporter with Adirondack Chronicles Magazine. She's interviewing me about the shop." He grinned, oblivious to the tension radiating from the server.

Nadia's expression soured further. With a narrowed gaze and pursed lips, she said, "The jelly beans." It wasn't a question.

"Yes, Nadia." Holly flashed a professional smile. "I'm here to learn about candy making, the town, and do a profile of Cal. I'm hoping to highlight other aspects of Bakersville in the three articles. I hope you'll let me interview you."

Her words broke the tension. Nadia stepped back, all hostility evaporating in a nanosecond. Her expression appeared leery, bordering on panicky. Her wide eyes darted around the room.

"You'd have to ask Mrs. Giovani. I don't..." She glanced around as if Holly had outed her as a spy. "I'll go get her." In a flash, the girl disappeared through the swinging tavern doors.

Holly laughed despite herself. "What was that?"

Cal grinned. "Just Nadia."

Holly ducked behind the menu, not wanting to alienate the townspeople by laughing at their antics. Bakersville was turning out to be a little weird.

After a minute, another presence haunted their table. Holly glanced up to find a short woman with salt and pepper hair glowering down at them.

"What's going on?" she asked in a thick Brooklyn accent. "You scaring off my servers?"

Thankfully, Cal stepped in. "No, no. Mrs. Giovani. This is Holly, here to interview me. She offered to talk to Nadia, too, but she spooked."

Mrs. Giovani picked up a menu and swatted Cal with it. "You know better."

Cal raised his hand in mock terror. "We didn't mean anything." His expression appeared contrite.

What was the story there? People either wanted to tell reporters their whole life or hide everything about themselves. Of course, the whole situation spurred her journalistic instinct to find out more.

Peeking over the menu cover, Holly raised an eyebrow at Cal. He shook his head. She shrugged.

She came to Bakersville for Cal, anyway. Including the townspeople might stretch the piece, but her editor wasn't interested in the life stories of twenty-somethings. Her curiosity sparked, and she made a mental note to ask more about the pizza shop.

"What do you want to drink?" Mrs. Giovanni glared at them, probably annoyed to be taking orders instead of Nadia.

"Do I even have to say?" Cal fluttered his eyelashes, and the woman blushed.

Holly studied the redhead sitting across from her. He held a certain charm, one that ran you over like a freight train, but charm, nonetheless.

"I only keep that crap here for you." She fluttered a hand and walked away without taking Holly's order.

Holly cocked her head, giving Cal a bit of a glare.

He smiled. "She does that sometimes." He slid out of his seat and headed for the drink cooler by the front counter. "What's your poison?"

Holly furrowed her brow. Caffeine would be necessary if she planned to spend a few days with the man. On the other hand, sugar might not be a good idea. "Diet iced tea?" she asked, hoping the case contained such an exotic drink choice. Well, exotic for such a mom-and-pop shop.

Cal flashed a thumbs up before spinning, executing a dancer's move to avoid a family of four, and landing at the cooler with a little leap.

Who was this guy?

As he opened the door, a sickening rattle filled the room. Everyone froze in their tracks. Cal stood, holding the door of the cooler. He raised his free hand while the rest of the restaurant patrons and staff held their breath.

The clattering culminated in an ear-splintering crack. The entire cooler lurched forward. Cal sprang into action, grabbing cans and bottles as they spilled from the shelf. He deftly plucked them from the air like a giant octopus.

One of the waiters dashed up behind him and stuck his hands inside the cooler.

"Got it, Asa?" Cal asked.

"Yep," he answered, and Cal stepped back. The bottles stopped dropping.

"Give me one second," Cal added as he deposited ten items on the counter. He slid under Asa and fiddled with the empty shelves.

Mrs. Giovanni stood by the counter, a firm scowl on her face. "Which one?" she asked.

"Shelf three, Mrs. G." Cal's head popped out from inside the cooler. "I got the support back in. It's a new one, right?"

With a sigh, the cook shrugged. "Damn thing. Every couple of days, another one breaks."

"It's the compressor, Mrs. G.," Asa said. "When it turns on, it shakes everything to death."

"Can you fix it, Cal?" Mrs. Giovanni wrung her hands.

Holly watched with interest. Cal was the candy maker, not the fix-it man. Or was he? A small town required people to wear many hats. She pulled out her notebook.

"Me, no. Not more than the band-aid fix. Again." He put an arm around the woman and pressed his head to hers. "Mrs. G, it's time. The cost of the mess every time a shelf breaks can't be worth it. We'll find a way to pay for it."

With a solemn expression, the woman let her shoulders drop. “As if I don’t have enough to worry about.” She threw her hands up. “Nadia! Get Cal his nasty diet cream soda and put these bottles in the back.”

As her resounding command faded, the restaurant returned to life with everyone talking and bustling around.

Cal spoke a few quiet words to Asa before returning to the booth.

“Does it happen often?” Holly asked once he sat down again.

Cal shrugged. “Often enough that I’ve gotten good at catching bottles.” He tapped his chin. “It always seems to wait for me. I’ve fixed it a dozen times. Anyway…” He waved his hands. “No worries. Hungry?”

Holly laughed. Keeping up with the candy man necessitated serious stamina. “Yes, what’s good?” She opened the menu again, perusing the usual list of Italian dishes.

Cal leaned across the table, “Can I be a total dick and order the food?”

Holly blinked. It wasn’t a date; it was an interview. “I guess.” Discomfort floated over her. She came here for business, not pleasure. And she didn't appreciate men overstepping and making decisions for her.

Yes, Cal's antics were entertaining, but…

"There are some secret menu items I can finagle out of Mrs. Giovani. Especially since I fixed the cooler again." He winked and waved Nadia over.

The woman sneered at him, crossed her arms, and shook her head.

He chuckled. "Guess my amazing save wasn't enough for Nadia." He slid out of the seat again and headed for the counter.

Nadia leaned her hip on the half wall and glared at Cal. Was she refusing to serve them? What kind of pizza place chose not to serve the customers?

Nadia and Cal probably had a history, but the age difference said not a romantic one. She resembled a college student in appearance and manner. Cal seemed to be closer to thirty and a better match for Holly.

And this isn't a date. She pulled in a breath and focused on the food.

The giant menu offered quite a few odd selections under Specialty Pizza. She's never heard of half of them—artichoke pesto, taco pizza, egg and sausage breakfast pizza, and the much-shunned Hawaiian.

Cal sat down with two cans of soda. "I put in an order and spoke with Nadia." He laughed. "She's opted not to wait on us."

Holly opened her mouth to ask why, but Cal cut her off with a gesture.

"Long story. Not a story for the papers. Anyway, I hope you like what I picked."

He popped open the can of Dr. Brown's and gulped down half of it. He raised it with triumph.

Holly wrinkled her nose, unable to hide her frown. She'd never cared for soda or any carbonated beverages, really. But diet cream soda? *Eww*.

Cal held out the can. "You sure you don't want any?" His teasing tone erased her grimace. "I'm eccentric." He lifted the can again as if posing.

"Ya think?" Holly twisted her lips into half a smile and jotted "eccentric" on her notepad. "Can we discuss my interview questions? You never answered my question about the chocolate."

Cal waved her off. "After we eat." As if on cue, Asa arrived with a large silver tray and stand. He arranged everything with precision, including plates, napkins, and silverware, and stood back. "On the house, of course."

"No, no," Cal sounded hurt by the gesture. "I only caught the bottles. Mrs. G needs the money for a new cooler. I promised Holly I would treat her to lunch."

Asa shrugged. "Aren't reporters supposed to wine and dine you. Put it all on an expense account." He nudged Holly's shoulder.

"What?" Holly hadn't been listening. Her attention focused on the pizza before them. The server arranged the six slices in a circle, each one a different type. White drizzle covered one slice. Shredded lettuce covered another piece. The third sported large, chunky circles of some vegetable. The other three were a complete mystery.

"Never mind. Pizza is much more important." Cal grabbed the server wedge and pointed to each piece in turn. "Chicken-bacon-ranch."

Ah, the white stuff looked like salad dressing, and on pizza?

"Red potato pizza, stolen from a shop in Willington, Connecticut." He moved to the next one. "Barbeque chicken and, of course, salad. That one is pickle, and the last is baked ziti. Pick your favorite!" He grinned as she poised over the tray.

"Is all the food like this?" she asked, trying hard not to wrinkle her nose. *What kind of Italian pizza place served potatoes on a pizza?* At home, the pies came in three flavors–cheese, pepperoni, and veggie. The choices here scared her.

Pickles on a pizza? She shivered.

His face sagged. "I wanted to show you the local color." He put down the server, his mouth in a serious pout. "I can get you a cheese slice."

Holly's heart lurched at Cal's expression. His excitement for everything bowled her over, but his disappointment pulled on her sympathies. She didn't want to make him feel bad for showing off his town.

"I guess I'll try the salad one or the one with the white gunk on it." It appeared tasty with a plain crust, tons of romaine, red onions, tomatoes, and peppers. A drizzle of dressing shone on the top, and Holly's stomach gurgled.

"Here," Cal said, gesturing over her head at the counter. Asa arrived in a flash with a pizza cutter and sliced each piece in two. After thanking the waiter, Cal slid the smaller of each new cut onto a plate and handed it to Holly.

"Just try a bite. You'll want to change your article over to Mrs. Giovanni's amazing cooking instead of my candy." He grinned.

Holly folded her arms. *The guy was such an odd duck.* "How is that good for your business?" she asked, sarcasm filling her words. She studied him, unsure of the entire situation. She came here to interview him and promote his candy shop. But they'd spent less than a minute inside. All of a sudden, he was pushing the pizza shop on her. What was his motivation? Callum McIntyre made no sense.

Cal shrugged. "I sometimes help with desserts. Oh, and I catch their falling soda bottles." His grin lit the room again. He nudged at her plate. "One bite and then I'll order a cheese."

Holly sighed and picked up the one with the white drizzle. No way would it taste good, and her stomach would scream at her for even trying it. But there was a job to do. If the guy refused to talk until she ate his weird pizza from his odd friends, she'd take one for the team.

Tentatively, she nibbled at the edge of the crust.

Cal threw his hands up. “You gotta do a whole bite and taste all the flavors.”

With a sigh and a roll of her eyes, Holly opened wide and took a proper bite. As she chewed, an explosion of flavors tickled her tongue. Her eyes grew wide. With her mouth full, she asked, “Which one is this?”

“It’s the chicken-bacon-ranch. Pretty amazing, huh? Try the red potato.” He tapped at the one with the chunky circles on top.

Never had she tasted pizza so delicious. It was as if they dined in a Manhattan pizzeria surrounded by the sights and sounds of a real city.

Real pizza in upstate New York.

Finally.

She made quick work of her first bite and selected the next slice. Again, flavor erupted in her mouth, but a wholly different kind of taste. The salty and starchy contrasted beautifully with the bite of the red sauce.

After she swallowed, she laid her hands on either side of her plate. “Oh. My. God. Cal.” She slapped her hand on the table with each word. “Does anyone know about this?”

He laughed, a full belly guffaw, and waved his hands at several framed reviews on the wall. "Award-winning, real New York City pizza." He leaned over the table conspiratorially, "You're welcome."

They sat in companionable silence as they finished the six slices. Holly, who usually had pizza with a cardboard crust, sweet sauce, and clumpy cheese, couldn't believe the pizza tasted amazing.

"You're right," she said with a grin. "There's a story here. Sorry, Cal. I'm ditching you for pizza."

He chuckled. "Well, I screwed that up. But…" He raised a finger. "You haven't tried my jelly beans yet."

Holly wrinkled her nose. "I don't like jelly beans."

Cal fell against the seat. "Then why did you come here? Geez, woman!"

Holly's face flushed with heat. Insert foot into mouth. Internal thoughts should stay internal.

"So…" Cal scrubbed his chin. "Possibly, you don't like jelly beans the way you *don't like* the pizza…" He winked, apparently his signature move, and relief flooded over her.

She glanced around the room. Could there be another story here? A whole exposé featuring the entire town? What other interesting tales slept in the tiny Adirondack town?

Cal reached over and grasped her hand, surprising her with his warm touch. “Just you wait. I have so much to share with you.”

Holly blinked.

Maybe it was a date.

Chapter Three

Pizza finished, Cal guessed Holly would pepper him with questions. He hoped he was ready to tell everything, and usually, he had no problem sharing every aspect of his life. He could be an open book for anyone.

Except that she started with the chocolate thing. Dread coiled in his belly.

"Great lunch." She flashed him with a knowing smile. "Now, about the lack of chocolate in your shop…"

Chocolate was not a topic for an empty stomach. With his belly full, he could spill a little of the story. He'd tell her everything if he knew his history would be safe with this woman.

He sighed, tossing his napkin on the table. “We stopped carrying it twenty-plus years ago.” He glanced anywhere but at Holly. Usually, he deferred to Suzanne or Wendy to tell the chocolate tale, but for the interview, they’d agreed he should be the one to share.

“So, here’s the big reveal for your article…” He pulled in a deep breath, steeling himself. She sat, pencil poised, and he took the plunge.

“I’m allergic to chocolate. I can’t eat it. I get hives, and my throat closes.” He peeked at her. Her pencil hung limply in her hand, and her mouth gaped open. He bit his lip.

In for a penny, in for a pound.

“I wouldn’t be able to taste anything I’d created with chocolate. Which doesn’t work well when you hand-make ninety percent of your stock.”

Holly leaned forward.

He raised a hand as if holding her back. The tension in his chest wound tighter. Time to add some humor, or he’d die of humiliation. “Suzanne and Wendy have volunteered to be taste testers, but it’s not the same.”

Holly responded with an "Oh." She looked at him, really stared. And the typical reaction hit her. "How can you…"

"You've seen the storefront. I've got an entire shop full of non-chocolate candies. I can bake any kind of sweet treat. I've created dozens of recipes. Most years, I'm in the black."

He slumped in his seat, some of the tension ebbing as he defended his position. "You can have a touristy candy shop in a mountain town without chocolate. I'm considering changing the name to 'No Chocolate Here.' You can use it for the article name."

Holly's brow furrowed. Her mouth twitched. She pulled in a breath as if to speak but stopped. She frowned, pointed a finger at him, and opened her mouth.

Nothing came out.

Same old reaction.

He sighed, ready to give the second part of his speech.

"No chocolate but many other goodies." He pulled on her hand, tugging her from the table. "Let's go to the shop. You need a few gumdrops or a meringue. You'll feel better."

"Okay, okay." As they neared the door, she pulled her hand away and waved the air clear. "No chocolate, because you are allergic. Couldn't you…?" She flapped her hands. "Seriously, the article is supposed to boost your tourism. I bet you'd hit the black every year if you sold…"

He crossed his arms over his chest. "Nope. Not gonna happen. Remember those rampant peanut allergies when we were little? A huge bunch of kids couldn't have peanuts in any form, and moms freaked out. Companies changed their labels, and warnings featured on every product." He held his hands out.

Silence hung in the air for thirty seconds. Holly blinked. "And?"

Oh, he never finished the thought. He'd talked for so long, he assumed… Scrambling, he retraced his argument.

Why did he talk about peanuts? …Oh, yeah.

He opened the door and ushered her onto the sidewalk. "So, yeah, they have to say if they have nuts in their factories, because it gets everywhere. Trace amounts of nuts can get into non-nut foods, and no one wants to be sued." He nodded, sure Holly would understand his point.

Her gaze narrowed as she studied him. A wave of discomfort rolled over him. Usually, people didn't study him closely. He swallowed hard, wondering if he sounded like an idiot.

"So," she said, tapping her chin as they walked along the main street. "If you use chocolate, there's a chance it will get into other products. For example, if you made chocolate fudge, it might end up in the vanilla fudge or the jelly beans?"

He clapped his hands and did a spontaneous jump.

She got it.

His reaction startled her, and she stepped away from him.

Okay, don't scare the woman.

He calmed his actions and spoke in earnest. "Consider cocoa powder. I can't touch it. Someone else makes cocoa crispy treats and doesn't clean well. Or they spill, and it's in the air. I touch it on the counter, or when I'm cleaning, then I get hives on my skin. Or I breathe it in, and I'm in the hospital. How would I make the candy if I'm on a respirator? No candy means we'd lose money by the fistful."

He shrugged. "So, no chocolate. Not now, not in the future. Not until Grandma takes the place back, but she won't do chocolate either. Maybe if I ever have a protégé and I retire or die." He shrugged again.

"It's a little dark. Okay, no chocolate. Weird, but okay."

It was his turn to blink at her. "Is it weird?"

She laughed. "Very. Anyway, it's also a selling point." She tapped her chin again. "You knew about the allergy at a young age?"

He wobbled on his feet, almost toppling them both onto the sidewalk. He needed to change the direction of their conversation.

With a furrowed brow, she reached for his arm. "You okay?"

He faked a smile but understood his expression revealed everything. "Can we go to the shop and sit in the kitchen? I need some familiar surroundings if I have to tell you the next part."

She nodded. Surprisingly, she wrapped her arm around his shoulder. "No worries."

What a nice gesture.

He probably looked like complete shit. Someday, he'd learn how to do a poker face. But apparently, not today.

They entered the front door, not bursting through at all. Suzanne hated it when he made a grand entrance, as she called it. Holly's arm slipped from his shoulder. It was almost a relief, but also a loss.

Inside, they found his manager and candy decorator, Wendy, deep in conversation. The discussion halted as Holly and Cal approached the counter.

Suzanne folded her arms and scowled at him.

"Hey Suzanne, this…"

She cut him off, as she did frequently. She had no patience for his ramblings. "Lunch?" she asked, her frown didn't budge. "And with the reporter due any minute, you take off and leave us hanging? Really, Cal…"

He cocked his head to the side and drummed his fingers on the counter top. Holly allowed him to ramble on, which was nice of her. Letting him run on sometimes helped him focus. Suzanne always cut him down, leaving a dozen strings of thoughts floating in the air like so much spaghetti.

Worried about what might come out of her mouth next, he forced himself to interrupt his manager. She hated when he did that, but he didn't deserve a public dressing down in front of Holly.

"Suzanne, Wendy, meet Holly Lincoln from Adirondack Chronicles magazine. We chatted over pizza, and I fixed the cooler again."

Suzanne's mouth snapped shut, and her grim expression disappeared like smoke. "I'm sorry I was rude." She dashed out from behind the counter, her hand out to Holly. "I'm Suzanne Hudson, manager here at McIntyre's Sweets. This is Wendy Miller, our sales associate. I'm pleased you could come visit us."

Cal stifled a giggle at his manager's abrupt mood change. But that was Suzanne, taskmaster with him and the employees—Wendy, and complete sunshine with the customers.

"Nice to meet you, Suzanne, Wendy," Holly's smile dazzled, and Cal found himself caught in her light and missed the exchange between the two women.

He'd tell Holly the rest.

Probably.

Maybe tomorrow.

Suzanne smiled at Holly. "Sorry we weren't here to greet you this morning. I'm sure Cal has everything under control. Are we doing a tasting or a demonstration today?" She pursed her lips and glared at Cal.

Yeah, he hadn't done either of those, but he would, eventually.

Wendy bit her lip, glancing worriedly between Suzanne, Cal, and Holly. He knew the look. What had he forgotten?

The air grew heavy as he racked his brain trying to remember. Wendy's eyebrows rose to her hairline. "The delivery?" she squeaked.

Suzanne spun, an expression of thunder on her face. Through gritted teeth, she said, "Can I talk to you in the back, Cal?"

Shit, he'd forgotten to drop off the order at the general store. The little grocery stocked a small selection of his more commercial candies. Since they were on the outskirts of town, the product placement was supposed to entice tourists to come into town proper and shop at his store.

The other merchants in town had similar items on the shelves, but his were featured on the front counter. Suzanne always pestered him to keep them stocked and ready. He understood on some level, but usually Suzanne's marketing plans usually went right over his head.

He mustered a half smile, which probably resembled a grimace. "Excuse us for a second, Holly. Suzanne and I gotta chat." Hopefully, he could hide his forgetfulness from Holly or ask her flat out not to put it in the article. He'd be allowed to read it before she published, right?

Suzanne tugged at his arm, and he realized he'd been off in his head again. "We'll be right back." He followed his manager into the kitchen, prepared to have his head handed to him.

Holly watched the two go, feeling confused. According to her miniscule research efforts, Cal owned the shop. Didn't he? The short blonde woman, Suzanne, seemed very much in charge. Holly turned to the willowy, dark-haired Wendy.

“Um,” Wendy said timidly, “don’t mind them. Suzanne is all bluster but has a big heart. Cal gets distracted sometimes.” She shrugged but folded into herself.

Holly turned on the young woman. She was petite, thin, and dark. Her enormous hazel eyes shone behind oversized glasses. *Ah, the decorator, time to chat her up.*

She turned her bright, reporter smile on the woman. “Wendy? You do the decorating? Tell me about it.”

Wendy’s face turned purple, and she ducked her head down. “I, uh, I thought the items needed a bit of color. The marshmallow thing, well, that got me into it.” She glanced at the kitchen door, and Holly understood the woman was trying to use her Jedi powers to get her coworkers to come back.

Holly leaned into the counter, ignoring the woman’s discomfort. Questions appeared to be difficult for Wendy. The article for her editor, Milton, required more depth than Cal dancing all over the place. “Tell me about the marshmallows.”

“Okay.” Wendy side-stepped the length of the counter as she spoke in a shaky voice. “Mrs. McIntyre creates these marshmallows. People love them. We dip them in caramel and other flavors…"

"But not chocolate?" Holly asked.

All the color drained from Wendy's face. "No." She shook her head vehemently. "No, never. Uh…" She took another few steps, and Holly mirrored her on the other side of the display cases.

"Mrs. McIntyre has these cookie cutters from June's shop. June is the antique dealer. Mrs. M cleaned them up and wondered what to make. She's not much of a baker, and she decided to use them on the marshmallows." Wendy took another step away from Holly.

Where was the girl going? And why would no one tell her more about the chocolate? There must be more to it based on everyone's reaction.

"Okay, cute shapes for the marshmallows. Like the chocolate-covered hearts for Valentine's Day."

Wendy stopped her side-stepping, her eyes wide. "No, no chocolate, only marshmallow." She blinked a few times, then cleared her throat.

Holly raised an eyebrow, and Wendy shot a glance at the kitchen door.

"Cal will have to tell you. We agreed he would do the telling."

Holly narrowed her eyes. She'd pull the details out of him before end of day. She'd dig up interesting tidbits for the article or die trying.

"Anyway," Wendy said, pulling a tray from the display. "The marshmallow shapes didn't make any sense on their own. The Christmas trees looked good with green dye, but the animals looked like lumpy clouds."

She held out a tray of sugary sweets in the shape of zoo animals. "I offered to decorate them, and they sold like hot cakes. We try to find cookie cutters for Mrs. M any time we are traveling. We have a good variety." She waved a hand at the rest of the marshmallow items.

Holly recalled the marshmallow treats from earlier with their delicate lacing across the front. "You decorated the egg ones, right?"

A slight blush rose on Wendy's cheeks. "I enjoy doing needlework, embroidery, and cross stitch. I thought the eggs for Easter might look nicer with fancy decorations. It's our first time selling these." She pulled out the tray of egg-shaped marshmallows. "Want to try one?"

Holly inspected the finely decorated item. The gold and pearls appeared to be real. "You can eat all the decorations?" she asked, confusion in her voice as she pointed to the fancy bits and bobs on the marshmallows.

Wendy smiled, seeming less shy. "Yes, the 'threads' are frosting. The pearls are sugar." She held one out for Holly in a gloved hand.

"Does Cal make the pearls?"

Wendy shook her head. "It's easier to buy them pre-made, but he makes almost everything else in the store. I…"

The kitchen door slammed open, and Cal strode out. Wendy's head ducked down, and she withdrew the treat.

Great, just when she had Wendy talking comfortably.

"Ready to go?" Cal asked. Both women turned to him.

"Where to?" Holly asked.

"General store. It'll take a sec."

"Fine," Holly grumbled, assuming she'd never hear the whole chocolate story. At this point, tasting the candy might be off the table, too.

Chapter Four

Holly followed Cal down the street, each of them lugging a plastic container filled with goodies. After a few blocks, they stopped in front of the local grocery store, if you could call it that. The outside of the building said General Store, and inside, a few food products lined the shelves. The store sported an array of touristy crap—t-shirts, mugs, and plastic snow globes.

And candy.

Does selling the candy in two spots actually help his store? Holly made a note to ask.

Inside, the store held old-world charm, with wooden shelves lining the walls and an open ceiling. She peered down the aisle and her brain slipped back to her childhood reading *Little House on the Prairie.* Every display, every shelf, every wall screamed small-town cuteness. The potential to catch the tourists appeared off the charts, but the goods catered to the town as well. The townies probably purchased their milk and bread here if a Stewart's Shop was too far a trip.

She followed Cal's lead and placed her container on the counter by the front register. No one appeared to be working. With a glance around the store, she asked, "You're going to leave…" She halted mid-sentence.

Cal had disappeared.

Holly wandered through a few stuffed aisles until she found him by the toys.

Of course.

"As a kid, I loved this place, but Grandma, not so much," Cal said, waving at a display of bright red packaging. "Those little cars, army men, dinosaurs. Every time Grandma brought me here, I begged for them."

"Okay." Holly glanced around. First a lunch date and then they ran out to do errands for the store. Why were they lingering here? Would it be like the conversation in the pizza shop and she'd get a few more tidbits of his story?

"Hey, Cal. Thanks for the delivery." A late twenties brunette with a cute haircut and even cuter nose paused next to them. She hooked a thumb at Holly. "Who's this?" Her apron sported the store logo, and the name Kinley was embroidered over her breast.

"Hey, Kinley. Meet Holly Lincoln, the reporter from the magazine."

Kinley furrowed her brow. "Huh, you must have forgotten to mention being interviewed for a big magazine." She ran a hand through her perfect hair and preened. "I'm not prepared for press, Cal." Her tone sounded both haughty and joking, obscuring the woman's meaning.

"No, oh, no." Cal slapped his forehead with one hand and held out the other to ward off Kinley. "She's doing a piece on the candy shop. So, I'm showing her some of my inspirations. You know…" He indicated the toys. "These guys."

"Ah," Kinley responded. "Whatever floats your boat, Callum." She turned to Holly with a roll of her eyes. "So, you here for the day or what?"

Holly glanced at Cal, then Kinley. He smiled with vigor but apparently didn't plan on any further introductions.

"Um, a few days. I'm staying at the B&B in town. I'm doing a feature about the candy store with some color from the town."

Kinley's brown eyes sparked. "So, you're doing the whole town? Cal didn't mention…" She fluffed her hair again. "He didn't say anyone would be staying here for days."

Here was a little more enthusiasm for her idea for a town-wide story. Her first impressions said Kinley desired attention. Sorry, Kinsley. The planned article would focus on Cal alone. But, if his shop turned out to be Boringsville, she'd say something nice about the general store and flood the article with pictures.

Kinley glanced around. "Hold on one second. I'll be right back." The woman dashed behind the counter and into a storage room. She ignored Cal's delivery at the register.

Huh. People here seemed a bit flighty. She turned to Cal, a bright smile on her lips. "How is this place your inspiration?"

He grinned. His crazy red hair and his lopsided smile dug into her heart more and more every time she saw his grin. He must have all the women eating out of his hands.

"I loved these toys." He pointed again to the packages of plastic bits. "I can't do chocolate, but I can make gummy candy and marshmallows. So, I created an entire line of gummy toy candy. I have army guys, sea creatures, Jacks, western-themed people." He wiggled his eyebrows, and Holly awarded him points for not saying Cowboys and Indians. "All fun flavors, even super sours. You can play first and eat after."

Kinley returned from the backroom with fresh makeup and a flush on her cheeks. "Okay, I'm ready."

Ah, someone wants a spotlight. Holly's editor didn't send her here to cater to the wishes of every shopgirl.

Attempting to remain professional, she asked Kinley, "How does it feel to inspire such an artist?"

Kinley's face fell. "Oh, my God. What a thing to say. Geez. It's not like that at all." She rolled her eyes. "We just sell the junk. Aren't you doing a spotlight on the store?" She fluttered her eyelids. "And me?"

"I'm sorry. The story is about Cal."

Kinley's eyebrows knitted together. "But you said…" She pointed at Holly. "And he said…" Red color crept up the woman's cheeks. "Why come here and tease me so horribly? Honestly."

The touristy store didn't fit the image the magazine wanted, but a picture of Cal and Kinley standing by the toys might work. "Can I snap a picture of the two of you by the toys? I'll contrast it with gummies in the article."

Kinley frowned, but Cal grabbed her hand and pulled her closer, posing in front of the red packages. The color clashed with his hair. Cal's grin spread ear-to-ear as he posed next to the toys. You would think he was showing the secrets of the universe. Next to him, Kinley pouted and posed, looking like a movie star with her perfect makeup and gorgeous hair.

Holly snapped off a few shots anyway. Either it would work or not—no use fighting it. She frowned. Maybe she wouldn't be able to use these photos after all. Having a beautiful woman hanging all over Cal in a photo, for her article… Holly blinked at the force of the jealous thoughts running through her brain.

Where the hell did that come from? She liked Cal but she wasn't interested in him. Or was she?

She needed to step back and quickly.

Today had been remarkable, being in such a weird little village with its cast of characters and their hyper candy man. Cal wasn't hers, and neither was the town. Who knew what kind of history these two had and what kind of person either of them were. Holly was here for a story, but not a love story.

Pictures taken, Holly thanked Kinley for her time and then followed Cal to the door.

He turned at the last second. "You going on the hike, Kinley? I'm gonna bring Holly along. Show her the mountain."

Kinley closed up again, arms crossed, a frown on her lips. "June might cancel with her bum ankle."

Cal shrugged. "You could always lead us. You know those trails like the back of your hand."

She rolled her eyes. It seemed the woman had two expressions—frown and eye roll. Never a grin when Cal flashed one.

Interesting.

Holly found the man's grin irresistible.

"As if you weren't the perfect lead, too. I mean, we grew up on those trails. Anyway, you might not wanna join us, Holly. It's real hiking, not a fashionable walk in the woods." Kinley lifted her chin as if in challenge.

"It'll be fine and fun. Hey, I left the delivery on the counter. Thanks for the pic, Kinley." With a wave, he dashed out the door.

Holly glanced at Kinley, whose mouth became a tight, solid line. Holly pitied the woman, stuck so far on the edge of town and unable to enjoy the light from a sun like Cal.

Cal sensed tension as he and Holly strolled to his shop. Not from Kinley and her desire for attention. The woman always seemed disappointed if the universe didn't praise her constantly. Of course, working in the remote shop and dealing with tourists didn't sound fun. He should find her another job. Something bright and sunny and visible.

He resisted sprinting back to his store. The staff, Wendy and Suzanne, were used to his dashing away for lunch at a random time between twelve and two. Suzanne always tisked at him, though. She was a task master with everyone. She never expected him to behave but asked him to, anyway.

He was lucky to have her as a manager.

"So," he said, pulling Holly along the sidewalk. "My grandma ran the store forever, and then she gave it to me. With the caveat, she gets to run the store when she visits."

"Hold up," Holly panted, "I don't have my recorder out. I need to take notes." She tugged at his hand. "Please, slow down."

Cal stopped mid-stride. "I know. I'm excited to tell you everything. We couldn't talk while we were eating, and you were chatting with Mrs. Giovanni afterward. She'll never give you any recipes, you being a reporter and all. And the soda cooler threatened again…"

"Stop," Holly said, her tone sharp. She pulled her hand from his. "I get you're all energy, but please complete one sentence before starting another. I can't follow you if we're walking and talking." She huffed. "Sorry. I'm not dressed for running around."

"Oh, man. I totally forgot about your shoes." He laughed. "Not that I'm into shoes or anything. Unless we're hiking. Do you hike? We have a trip planned…"

Holly raised her hand again.

Cal stuttered to a stop. The woman made him nervous—pure business, all big city style and manners. If she'd never had good pizza, she couldn't be from The City.

He paused for a long blink, a coping technique he'd learned at a young age. Blink, breathe, think. She asked him to slow down and stop rushing. Not the best time to invite her to go hiking.

"Sorry," Heat rose on his cheeks, and his pale skin burned with embarrassment.

She jutted out a hip and flashed him a cool look. "You gonna ever tell me about the chocolate thing?" she asked as they passed the Antique Shop.

"That's June's store. You can meet her if we go on the hike." He pointed across the street. "And there's the bookstore. They have a counter for coffee but no snacks." He spun as he walked. "And there's the Penny Saver office. They're open a few days a week."

A hand pressed on his arm, tugging him to a stop. Holly stood and gazed deep into his eyes. "You don't have to tell me the rest of the chocolate story if you don't want to. You also don't have to deflect by taking me to every store on Main Street." She waved an arm at the other shop fronts. "I'm sure you have a lovely town here. But I'm supposed to interview you. If it's not okay, we can talk about it."

Cal turned and stood in front of her. He liked this direct woman and loved how she saw through his antics. He wanted to know more. "Did you ever watch that old movie with the serial killer?"

Holly blinked at him, her hand dropping to her side. "What now?"

Cal chuckled. "The one with the guy in the jail cell and the young FBI agent. The title has farm animals…"

"*Silence of the Lambs*?" Her eyebrows bunched together, and her mouth hung open. Not the first time his thought processes thoroughly confused someone.

"Yes! That's the one. What's the line? '*Quid pro quo*, Clarise.'" He waggled his eyebrows.

"You're creepy." Holly pushed past him and headed to his store.

He caught her arm, stopping her. "No, I meant… I'll tell you stuff about me, and you tell me about you."

She crossed her arms over her chest. "Cal, do you know how interviews work? I ask you questions. You answer. That's it."

He shrugged and resumed strolling down the sidewalk. "Since we had so much fun at lunch, we should talk more."

Holly sighed as she caught up with him. "Lunch was nice. I've never tasted pizza that good outside the city." The weight of her gaze pressed on him, but he refused to look at her. "I might be persuaded to chat more. We'll see."

A bubble of excitement built in Cal's chest. She said she'd tell him more about herself and possibly go on the hike. He resisted a fist pump as they arrived at his shop. What he needed to do was create something special for Holly.

To deflect some of the bubbling, he said, "My brain jumps on whatever path reveals itself. Anyway. Come inside, and we'll do all that interview stuff—talk, test the candy, talk more…" He grinned, mulling over what to create for someone who didn't like jelly beans.

All other thoughts disappeared as his mind focused on a new creation. Once inside the store, he'd let Wendy and Suzanne take the reins for a bit while he whipped up that thing for Holly.

He tuned back in as Suzanne, with a slick smile gliding over her lips, said, "Why don't you two go in the kitchen and talk candy, and I'll get everything ready." She patted Cal's hand and tipped her head toward the door.

Get what ready?

Cal shrugged. "Let's begin again. Come on into my kitchen and see where the magic happens."

Holly followed behind him into the kitchen. "I thought we already agreed there's no magic in your beans." She nudged him. "Are you lying to me?"

"We agreed they *were* magical." He scrubbed his neck as he pulled out a stool at the worktable and patted it for Holly.

"Maybe you should slow down when you talk."

Once they were both seated at the counter, Holly removed the notebook and recorder again. "Okay, take two. Tell me about your shop."

Cal grinned, "You ready?"

Holly leaned in. "Hit me."

For the next ten minutes, Cal recited a fast-paced history of the shop. How his grandparents started out with Grandma as the master candy maker. He skipped over his parents' deaths, cutting to the part where Gramps and Grandma took him in and taught him the business.

"So, never a question about you taking over for them?" Holly doodled a note on her paper. Cal noticed she doodled tons of little drawings over the page, contrasting with notes in tight, clipped handwriting.

"Oh, I was all over the place for a bit. I worked here as a teen, learned to create jelly beans and other sugary sweets, but I couldn't focus on one career. Grandma and Gramps let me try everything. From about sixteen on, I hung out at the diner, the firehouse, and the gas station. I worked a few jobs with a blacksmith, as a hotel bellhop, and as a salvage guy at the local recycling facility. Every time, I came home. The candy called me back."

Holly grinned, her smile burning into his chest. “That’s a great story.”

A thrill ran through him to think he’d impressed a sophisticated lady with his goofy, hyper self. She probably had ten guys lined up at home. But for the next three days, he’d enjoy her company.

“So, you’re a jack-of-all-trades?” she asked, making a note. Their eye contact broke, and Cal found himself struggling to catch her gaze again.

“Nah, I can fix a shelf or repair a small engine. I’m a baker of sorts–all chemistry and mathematics. You need a certain kind of brain to do the work. You have to problem-solve a lot. Some days, like with spring and holidays, the job gets rote, but I gotta work to make enough to sell, have a profit, and keep my customers happy.”

“Is that the crux of it, Cal?”

He did another slow blink. Every time she said his name, his heart raced. Which was stupid because he had just met her, but she seemed exciting. A new face and not a tourist. Her smile, her eyes, those legs… A career woman from a city with a whole…

“Cal?”

He broke off his random thoughts and tried to focus. “Yeah?”

“What was your smile about?”

He sat back, straightening. “What smile?”

Holly glanced at her notes and back at him, a sparkle in her eyes. “I asked about the crux of your business, and you wandered off. Where’d you go?”

A light sweat broke out over him. No one challenged him on his brain fogs. Everyone in town either ran over his pauses or cut through his rambling speech. He didn’t know how to answer with anything but the truth.

“I was thinking about you.”

Holly gaped at him, her pen faltering in her hand. “I’m sorry. I …”

“Here we go.” The kitchen door burst open, and Suzanne marched into the room. She held an open assortment box. “As promised. Taste what he can do.”

Cal pressed his lips at Suzanne’s awkward wording.

The woman continued without a hitch. “Don’t let him fool you with his humble act. Cal is a master at his craft. Any of these would win him awards.”

Oh, Jesus. Thank God for Suzanne.

Cal had almost asked Holly back to his place.

"Thank you so much," Holly said to Suzanne, grateful for the woman's timing. Holly kept getting lost in Cal's musings, staring at his handsome face and the red hair. It looked like frozen fire, and she desperately wanted to run her hands through it.

Holly swallowed hard and focused on the tray of candy before her. A dozen different sugar confections shone from the little box. She came here to interview the man. Nothing more. No one-night stands, no quickies in the candy shop. And an interview, simple enough.

Suzanne stood between them, hands on her hips. When Cal cleared his throat, the manager seemed to understand the message. "Oh, well, I'll leave you two alone." With a bob of her head, she moved back into the store.

"All right," Holly said, drawing the words out. She glanced over the goodie box and pointed to the circular, sugary bites with elaborate designs inside them. "Tell me about these."

Cal picked up a pink cylinder with a bunny in the center. “These are called sticky candy. Silly, right? Nah, that’s the name of the company that invented them. They are basically cut rock candy. I create my own spin with themes of shapes and flavors. The kids love ’em. Probably because I give out samples by the hundreds.” He grinned.

“Doesn’t it cut into your profit margin?”

He shook his head. “Nah, gets the kids excited. And the parents buy a bunch. It’s advertising.”

Holly grabbed one. She popped the candy in her mouth and blinked at him. “What is this flavor? I…” She tapped her chin, considering.

“Bubble gum.” He shrugged. “The kids love it. Anything pink ends up cotton candy-ish or bubble gum.”

Holly savored the sweet, regretting she’d picked a hard candy. She’d have to finish it before sampling another.

Cal appeared to read her mind. “Here. Spit it into a napkin.” He passed one over. “It’s a tasting, right? They do that with the wine, don’t they?”

Holly lowered her eyes, embarrassed to spit in front of someone. “Seems like a waste.”

He waved her off. “Nah. I can get you a cup if you want to save it.”

“No, it’s fine.” With little sophistication or daintiness, she spat the candy into the napkin and placed the mess on the table.

“How about this one next?” He handed her a small, wrapped roll resembling a piece of sushi. “For these guys, I roll the candy and cut it, like sushi. Instead of fish, it’s made with puffed rice and salted taffy.”

Holly picked up the faux roll and studied it. “Can I bite it?”

A smile turned up Cal’s lips. “Small bites. It’s intense.”

Holly sampled a corner. The rice and taffy mixed on her tongue. “Delicious.” The intensity of sweetness and the rich flavor had her mouth watering for more.

“I create different types of these guys for different holidays. Traditional foods, but the candy version.”

Holly nibbled the rice treat again, unable to resist the sweet treat. “Do they sell well?”

Cal shrugged. “I never have extra when I do a run for a holiday. A couple of times a year, I get special requests. I try to work with whatever people want. Like these guys…"

He waved at a row of shapes on the tray. A mother otter held a baby. Next to it, two otters held hands. They were constructed of a gel-like material but were not gummy bears.

Holly lifted a gray lump. "What's this?"

Cal delicately lifted a second candy. "These are from my Australian line. Yours is a koala. This one's a platypus. I did a whole series of candies during those fires a few years ago. For every bag, I sent half the profit to a fund to help the people and animals there." He grinned and popped the platypus in his mouth. "Try it."

She did. It tasted like a traditional gummy bear, but different. The flavor sang on her tongue, but she couldn't place it. "Okay," she said, after chewing thoroughly. "What's the catch? These are not what I expected."

Cal tossed a kangaroo back. "Besides the cool shapes and being homemade?" He shrugged. "I can't spill all my secrets. It's in the recipe."

Holly selected a minuscule candy and studied it. "Kiwi?" she asked and put it in her mouth. *Yep, it tasted like its name. Smart*. "Show me how you make these?"

"But you're here for my jelly beans." He touched the boxes with various colored and sized bean-shaped candies. "That's what your people asked about specifically."

She fiddled with her pen for a moment. "My people will want the entire story. So, you mentioned quid pro quo. Tell me about the chocolate." She winked, using his quirk to grab his attention.

Cal swallowed hard.

The two stared at each other in a stalemate. Obviously, there was more to the chocolate thing than he was ready to share. She'd wait to push him. She'd finish the candy tasting, then the cooking demo as promised. Tomorrow would be soon enough. Especially since he wanted some of her personal info, too.

Cal's mouth remained closed for once, and she refused to offer anything personal without the complete story.

Chapter Five

"I already told you my secret," Cal rubbed his lips, "Tell me yours."

Holly lifted an eyebrow. "Being allergic to chocolate is your big secret? Really?"

Again, she called him on his bullshit, but how else was he supposed to transition into learning about her as a person?

He studied her for a second over the tasting tray. "Why did you want to be a reporter?"

She put down the tiny meringue she was about to sample. "Journalism is essential." Her words sounded stilted and cold, not a bit of passion firing behind them. “Reporters are important people.”

Huh.

He understood on a basic level that not everyone worked in their dream job, nor did they have his type of passion for work. Her answer sounded as if she didn’t enjoy being a reporter.

“Yeah,” he said, “super important. Look at what your article will do for my shop. I bet we get a ton more visitors. Your magazine has a pretty wide distribution and…”

Holly’s eyes narrowed. “I’m aware of what type of media outlet I write for. It’s a stepping stone. Once I have some stellar references and better writing chops, I’ll get a real journalism job.”

Cal’s mouth hung open. Passion spiced her words, but bitterness did as well. “I wasn’t saying…”

Holly snorted. “I’m aware I’m the queen of puff pieces. I write about dog shows and pie-eating contests. Once a paper or news outlet finally notices me, I’ll have an actual career.”

Cal popped a jelly bean in his mouth and chewed it slowly to collect his thoughts. *Quid pro quo* indeed.

Holly might not have realized how much tea she spilled, and he wanted more.

"So, you want to work for a big paper or a news channel. That's super cool."

She huffed. "I want to be a war correspondent. Do something with a real impact on other people. I wasn't raised to be a small town nobody, writing stories about quilting circles and winter fairs." She tossed her braid over her shoulder and crossed her arms.

Was she trying to convince him or herself?

Cal poked a little more. "War correspondent? Wow, that sounds terrifying. Do you have a lot of experience with combat zones? I'm not sure I could handle anything so intense."

"Well…" Holly turned her body sideways, crossing her legs, her nose in the air. "Not directly, but I could do it. I'm a talented writer, and I understand how to dig into the heart of any story. I could do amazing things in the field. The real field."

Cal reached out a hand. Holly seemed to be too vulnerable here, and he didn't want to pull a Hannibal Lecter and scare the crap out of her. Or allow her to believe he felt insulted by her implying his store was a minor story.

He touched the tips of her fingers under her clenched arms. “You would be amazing. I can’t wait to watch you on CNN.”

She pulled away from his touch, uncrossing her arms and blinking rapidly.

Shit, he made her cry. He never meant to be a dick, but here he was again making the women cry.

“You think I could report on CNN? You just met me. My parents don’t believe I can do CNBC.” She brushed at her eyelashes.

Cal handed her a napkin, but not the one with a half-eaten candy. “I’ve known you about six hours, and you’ve impressed me as an intelligent woman who gets what she wants. You’re going places, Holly Lincoln.”

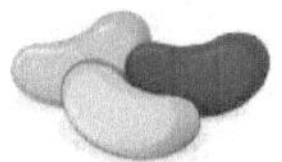

Who was Callum McIntyre?

Holly stared at her shoes, her too-high, fancy, mauve shoes. She’d dressed for a city interview—neutral colors (her favorite) and a smart pantsuit. She hadn't brought much for running around a small town like some fanatic. And a person she just met gave her the biggest ego boost of her life.

Her ambitious parents did nothing but criticize her for every career choice. They pushed and pulled her, driving her goals ever higher, currently landing on international war correspondent. She'd jumped at the idea without a backward glance.

They always demanded that she do things, never encouraged or inspired. She was merely told she *would* do it, and right now. This man, who knew she wrote the *Puppy Report*, told her she was amazing. How was that possible?

She studied him. Perhaps he did know. He said he loved her work. Or maybe he was trying to get into her pants.

She met his eye, and he blushed a little. *Ah, the pants angle*. Oh, well, they seemed to have chemistry, a connection between them, but it appeared to be purely physical. Holly could only count on herself. She'd write a phenomenal story, win a prize, and make her parents proud of her.

"So," Cal began, bringing Holly back to the present. "Did you want to try the jelly beans or do more of the other candies? Are we doing a cooking demo? I planned to make fresh jelly beans, well, a few of the steps for it, but if you don't want to, we could always…"

Holly raised a hand, tickled by his inability to edit himself. "I'm here for the beans, so let's do it." She gazed over the selection in the tray, picked up one, and placed it in her mouth.

Jelly beans were not at the top of her list, but she chewed carefully, remembering his wine tasting reference. A gush of flavor hit her mouth as her teeth sank in. She placed a hand over her mouth, surprised and worried she'd spill.

"What?" she sputtered.

"Ah, my flavor-filled beans. Like those fruit snacks from when we were kids. What do you think?"

Holly chewed, not tasting, being too surprised at the rush of liquid to appreciate the candy. "Let me try another."

"One at a time," he cautioned and handed her another bean. "Lemon. Nice and neutral."

She flashed the stink eye at him for half a second

before popping the bean. Slowly, she sank her teeth into the candy.

Cal grinned and sounded a clap. "You've got it. Slow and steady. Appreciate the flavor."

In that instant, Holly's whole world centered on her mouth. The taste froze her in place.

The candy's flavor morphed beyond plain old lemon to the sweetest, sourest lemonade, sipped on a hot day.. The rich flavor filled her mouth, and she released a little groan. If all of Cal's jelly beans were as delicious as the first one, she could grow to love them.

"These must be the reason my editor sent me here. He'd gushed"—Holly groaned at her terrible pun—"about the specialty flavors and unique beans." She held up a green one. "I bet these are the ones that enamored my boss."

"Not bad, huh?" he smiled. This time, his grin seemed sheepish. "I've had good feedback on those."

Holly ate another one. The pure cool sensation of lime washed over her. She closed her eyes and lived in the flavor. How did he fit so much punch in a jelly bean?

"My god, Cal." The words came out with a moan. "They're like crack."

He chuckled. "Oh, wait until you try these." He selected another bean, a little larger than the first set. The color shone a dusky brown.

She eyed him but accepted the candy and did another slow chew.

"Whoa," she said, her eyebrows rising to her hairline, and the smooth, warm sensation of the flavor rolled over her tongue. "Is it…?" She had no words. She, the reporter, the woman who'd already clocked a million words in print, could not find the simple name of the flavor in her brain.

Cal picked up a matching bean. "Yep, from our 'Adult Line.'" He waggled his eyebrows. "A little Jim Beam, in a bean. Get it?" He winced at his own pun and hurried to explain. "These are for twenty-one and over customers. They come complete with a finger-wagging explanation from Suzanne." He selected another and considered it. "By the time these guys are cooked and set, no alcohol is left. But we take no chances."

Holly swallowed the lump of candy with a hard gulp. "You put booze in the jelly beans?"

Cal shrugged. "They do it for chocolates. Why not beans?"

Holly stared at him, speechless when the realization hit. She knew nothing about candy making, styles, trends, or anything. She'd failed the assignment. Hadn't he mentioned this before lunch? To hide her addled thoughts, she pushed the topic. "Tell me more about your 'Adult Line'?" She smirked to keep the air light but the topic could be add some substance to the article.

Cal's face flushed purple. "Oh. My. God. No. Not that kind of adult line." His gaze dove for the floor, and he refused to look at her. "We don't have anything like that. The liquor beans are the sole 'adult'"—he made air quotes around the word adult—"items in the store. I never… No… I couldn't… God." He blushed harder, bright enough to make his head explode.

They sat in silence for a few seconds before a chuckle escaped her lips. Holly could bet they were both picturing the same thing, his grandmother and some saucy cookie cutters for the marshmallows. Their gazes met, and both burst into laughter. Cal laughed so hard, he practically fell to the floor. Once they calmed, they gazed at each other over the countertop.

"I…" he began.

Another flush of excitement rolled over Holly's skin.

At that moment, the kitchen door swung open, and Suzanne stepped in. She tapped her watch. "Cal, we have that order…" She glanced between the two of them, disapproval darkening her expression.

"Yes. Um, yes. Okay." He stood glancing from Holly to Suzanne.

Who was in charge here?

Cal ducked his head. "See, we are trying an online store, and the growing pains are enormous. Packing and shipping are a pain." He glanced at his watch. "I try to do them at the end of the day. Do you mind?" His cheeks held the slightest tinge of pink.

"Um, no. It's fine." The air in the room changed, and Holly wondered if they'd missed a moment.

Cal bit his lip, disappointed about Suzanne's rotten timing. Twice in one afternoon, too. She acted like his mother half the time, but today, it felt a little much. He'd have to speak to her about bossing him around in front of a reporter.

Especially this reporter.

He had no idea if what stirred between them was romance, lust, or Holly's flirty ways. He didn't care. He was into Holly, and why not pursue it? But not if Momma-Suzanne planned to slap him down every time.

"I also have to whip up a few batches of jelly beans to replace the items sold this week. I like it better when Easter is late. I sell so many more beans. No one wants to buy jelly beans in February." He pressed his lips, realizing he was rambling.

Holly smiled but glanced at her phone, noticing the time. "I'd love to watch you work, but it's late. How about tomorrow morning? It would add great depth to the article. Any chance for a recipe I can share?"

Both Suzanne and Cal shook their heads. Promo was one thing, sharing family secrets was another.

Suzanne jumped in over him. "You can't publish any of his recipes. That wasn't part of the deal." She wagged a finger at Holly, who stepped back, her eyes wide. "You're…"

Internally, Cal sighed. *Here went Suzanne again—bossy, bossy, bossy.* With as much calm as he could manage, he gripped Suzanne's finger and slowly lowered her hand, cutting her off mid-rant.

"Holly understands our deal. Images and descriptions and interviews. No recipes." He flashed a smile at Holly but lowered his gaze to Suzanne. "Right?" He asked the question more to his manager than to the reporter.

Suzanne sighed. "I know, but these city-slickers…"

His gaze met Holly's, and they both burst into laughter.

Holly covered her mouth and said, "Don't worry, Suzanne. I have ethics. I didn't realize how long we've been chatting. I have to check into the inn for the night." She lowered her hand to reveal a professional smile, no malice or teasing, though her eyes still danced a bit.

He could get used to the gleam in her gaze.

"Are you staying in Lake Placid or the B&B?" Suzanne asked.

Holly glanced between them, as if Suzanne dared to ask about her and Cal's romantic situation. He should've asked her to stay with him. Then he'd cook her dinner and …

Holly broke through his intrusive thoughts. "The B&B. I assumed if I stayed in town, I could drink in the atmosphere. I'm going to go over my notes before I head over and check in."

Cal exchanged a look with Suzanne. He'd probably have to help in the end. Russ was a great guy, but he struggled with the Inn. Everything in his being said, "Offer to help her get settled" but he could see from the weary look in her eyes, she needed a break.

"Until tomorrow, then," he said, trying not to sound wistful.

Chapter Six

Holly opted to escape town for dinner. Another meal with Cal might have been lovely, but she needed to send a rough draft to Milton, her editor, before midnight tonight. Her three-day stay might depend on her ability to make the travel expenses worthwhile.

Hunkered down at a fast-food place near Sacandaga Lake, she typed a quick summary of her day and the town. Or was it a village? Again, the lack of research kicked her butt. She attempted to capture the aura of Bakersville without making it sound like Mayberry.

It wasn't working.

Her summary appeared…well, thin. Her experience in Bakersville was anything but.

Tossing out the scant paragraphs, she opted to write the actual article. Not what Milton wanted, but her work flowed better if she just sat down and pounded it out. Editing a finished article was much easier than redoing a summary.

Once she finished the preliminary piece—an intro and a description of the town, store, and the handsome Cal—she emailed Milton and focused on finishing the large plate of French fries she should not have purchased.

Five minutes later, her phone pinged with a video call. *Ah, Milton, working all the hours again, huh?*

His ruddy, round face appeared on the screen. His salt and pepper mustache hiding his expression. His bushy eyebrows said frown. He didn't mince words but went straight for the jugular. "Your article needs more spice."

Holly frowned. "It has spice. I put the crap Cal told me about his candy in there. I did the atmosphere thing. What more do you want?" She tried to hide her grimace. In her opinion, the article sat this side of perfect. It contained all the elements needed, only lacking details she could get tomorrow. A few more sweeps and she'd be in the clear.

Bakersville was growing on her, but no way she'd admit it. She wanted out and away from the brilliant, adorable Callum McIntyre. Everything he did seemed fun and interesting. She didn't have time or inclination to cultivate the relationship.

Milton broke into her thoughts. "Look, Holly. You're an excellent writer, but there's more here. Get to know the guy and make the piece sing."

She sighed. Not the answer she wanted. She hoped her original puff piece would turn off her editor and make him send her home, away from temptation.

Apparently not.

"You're right in the mountains. Get some color. It's spring. Visit the surrounding area and add atmosphere. With what you've sent me, have you considered doing the entire village? A multi-piece exposé of sorts. We can talk to the town officials, have the piece syndicated…"

Milton prattled on, but Holly tuned him out. A syndicated piece sounded amazing, but about such a Podunk town? Ugh, her crime-byline dreams shriveled before her.

"I'll see what I can do," she mumbled. Would another paper take a chance on a cub reporter? She wanted television, real press, authentic stories. With everything digital these days, her hopes of being a reporter for a large newspaper shrank by the day. Small-town papers no longer existed.

"Holly," her boss's voice sounded sharp. "I already called ahead. So be there."

Her attention snapped back to the video call. "What?" Panic crept over her skin. Did she miss something?

Milton's loud laugh brayed like a hyena. The jokester got her again. "You have a far-off look when you space out on me." He wagged a finger. "I get it. It ain't your dream job. Welcome to the club. I'm giving you a chance here. Take it."

She swallowed hard. "So… Be where? When?" She flashed a tight smile, hoping to quell any anger.

He laughed again. "I didn't make any appointments for you, but stop by their little local press… It'd be worth your while." He grinned and cut the call off. Within a minute, an email arrived with a list of items to either research or write about.

Damn, Milton and his 150 words a minute. He still held the paper record.

She glanced over the list. More about the candy shop, do local activities, visit the town's press, eat at the local stops, and send an article on each.

With resignation and a deep level of exhaustion, she set to work researching the town. After a couple of hours, she retrieved her lame article and worked on the revisions and outlines for the other two articles Milton requested. She arrived back in Bakersville exhausted, overworked, and outrageously late for check-in.

In her room at the B&B, Holly thanked the manager, a thirty-something black man in large-framed glasses, one more time before closing her room door. She peered through the peephole, and he remained standing outside the room.

His deeply furrowed brow and twitchy lips said he was nervous. But nervous about what? Holly wondered if she should invite the guy in to chat for a bit. Before she could, the man wandered off down the hall.

Maybe she should call Cal to…

She dismissed the idea. She didn't require a man to save her from an overworked night manager. She didn't need to solve all the problems of the world tonight. It was late, which was probably why the man seemed off. She'd probably woken him, or he was worried she'd bailed on her reservation.

With a deep sigh, she leaned against the door. *What a day*! She'd delivered the product, eaten, and toured the town. She had good research under her belt and three solid outlines. She'd scrapped the first draft of the article. She wanted the piece to shine, and the right spotlight on Cal would do it.

But where to begin, and where to finish?

At first, it sounded easy. She'd meet the candy guy, talk to him, watch him cook, and write it up afterward. Instead, she received a world tour of Bakersville, NY, along with meeting half a dozen people and partaking in the best pizza she'd ever eaten.

And Cal…

Man, oh, man, the guy threw her for a loop. He had the vigor of a cheetah on energy drinks. He'd never stopped once the entire day. Well, he did have a few long pauses to think. She could tell his mind raced every time he tapped his lip or his expression became dreamy. The man had ideas and a giant labyrinth of a brain.

How did the man's girlfriend keep up with him?

Did he have a girlfriend?

He seemed flirty with her, but it might be that the super charming, small-town, all-around good guy atmosphere he emitted had something to do with it. Yes, she needed that many adjectives to describe him. Any less would diminish the man and his boundless energy.

She flopped on the bed face down. Cal had run through ideas for tomorrow's activities. Making a batch of jelly beans together would be best. Doing so would give her "a real understanding of the process." Next, he wanted her to meet his grandmother for the history of the candy shop. Last, he wanted to go on a hiking trip with a group of townies.

"We planned it a while ago, and I forgot when we scheduled the interview. I thought about the view from the top of the mountain. Well, not the top. Whiteface is close to five thousand feet. We're doing a simple hike because June is on the mend from a bad ankle."

Holly was getting used to his run-on conversations. "June? The antique store owner you mentioned?"

Cal pointed down the street. "Yeah. She and my grandma are besties. She's not as young as she used to be. Poor thing. She hurt her ankle about a week back, which is why we changed the date of the hike and the venue and the difficulty level…and…"

"How did she hurt herself?" Holly pictured a Miss Marple-type with white curls and a cane she used to whack people as much as lean on.

"She crashed her Harley. She was pissed because she'd just had it detailed." Cal shrugged as if sixty-year-old women driving motorcycles was a regular thing.

Not in Holly's world.

She considered the conversation as she lay flat on the bed. She wanted to meet June. The story contained plenty of color with the plan to highlight the town. The copy in her head resembled an exploding box of sixty-four crayons with one hundred and twenty crammed inside.

She rolled on her side. She could make a career of writing pieces about the town, even having only been to the candy shop, the pizza parlor, and hearing about the antique store. What were the chances Milton would allow her to stay and…

The idea made her sit up wide awake. Stay in this Podunk little town?

Perish the thought.

She'd never become a star reporter for any paper or any real news agency writing about small-town drivel.

She flopped over, chagrined for dissing the cute little town. She arrived here to complete one job, and hell, she already had enough for the five columns.

Closing her eyes, she savored the softness of the bed. Not her job, not her town, but the place was nice, the bed felt soft. She'd stay for the three days and get the story. If she enjoyed good food, amazing candy, and the company of a charming redheaded man, she'd just have to endure it.

Her eyes closed, and she dreamed of gummy animals.

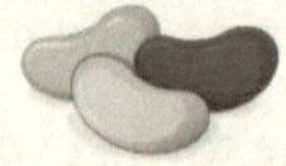

Cal wiped the counters for the tenth time. He never kept the shop open late, but he wanted to show Holly everything. They'd gotten a late start. The pizza lunch threw them off schedule. Of course, there were the questions and sampling and filling orders without Holly. He'd planned to do a cooking demo today, but they never seemed to finish the task.

With a sigh, he checked the stove. He always checked all appliances at the end of each day. After, he scanned the walk-in fridge and pantry. Everything appeared to be ready for the next day.

He'd create beans with her tomorrow. They'd do the regular, the cream-filled, and the liquid-filled. He wished he'd say something interesting or new to share for the article. Nothing sold candy better than novelty.

Just like the golden ticket movie…

He tapped his chin. *Perhaps a jaw breaker…*

The kitchen door opened, and Suzanne slumped in the doorway.

"What are you still doing here?" she asked, before he did.

"I didn't show Holly how to make any candy creation. I have a plan for the morning, but I'm missing something. I wanna go on the hike and have her meet my grandma."

He planned to go on, but Suzanne always interrupted him. Didn't she understand yet that talking helped him process? Otherwise, he got lost in his head. Hearing his own words focused him.

"You can do it tomorrow. If you want to take more time off for a hike, we need to talk about the books before you go."

Cal waved her off. At this hour, he had no desire to discuss finances. Keeping it together all day for Holly had burned his circuits. He needed some good food and a full night's sleep before he could talk money.

"I didn't take time off today. We had everything planned. Stocked and ready to roll." He waved around the immaculately clean kitchen, proud he'd planned ahead so well.

"Except you took a long lunch, and I never got a break." She huffed and folded her arms over her chest.

Cal didn't want to get into it tonight. Suzanne was notorious for "forgetting" to take a break and complaining later. She only had to mention she wanted lunch or dinner or whatever before walking out the door. He ensured he could help at the counter at any time. He took a lunch break about once a week. Cal made Suzanne aware that he and Holly would be an all-day-long thing before the reporter arrived.

But he loved Suzanne like a sister or aunt, family anyway. He'd say nothing and let it go, as he did every other time. Who else would do his books so perfectly, if not Suzanne?

"Sorry. Crazy day. Tomorrow won't be any different. I do wanna go on the hike to show Holly the region. It's a shorty because June is still hurting."

Suzanne's gaze sparked fire. *Ah, the perfect distraction.* Suzanne and June appeared to have some sort of rivalry. Hell, they'd lived in the same town for over fifty years. Of course, they had history.

Big history.

"June needs to understand her limits. A Harley? What was she thinking? Those things are heavy. My Suzuki Boulevard is much more practical."

Suzanne huffed again when Cal failed to jump on the motorcycle topic. "Anyway, you can swing the short hike if you finish the demo. I need you to refill two days' worth of candy here. People are stocking up for the holiday." She wagged a finger as if she owned the store. "I don't want profits to dip because you're chasing a pretty face."

Cal's jaw dropped. *Chasing a pretty…?*

"Whoa, whoa, whoa." He pursued Suzanne through the storefront. "I am not after Holly. She's a reporter. She's going to write about my life, my store. I have to be nice."

Suzanne pulled open the front door and motioned him out. "Nice? You've gushed over her from the beginning. Really, Cal. She's pretty, but the stick up her ass needs to be surgically removed."

The statement stopped him mid-stride. "She's not uptight. She's working."

"Yeah, right," Suzanne scoffed as she double locked the door. "She didn't chill out when you fed her jelly beans."

Cal blinked, considering Suzanne's words. The scene in the kitchen replayed in his head. Holly's eyes sparkled, amazed over the taste of the whiskey beans. No stick was present as far as he could see. Of course, Suzanne hadn't spied on them the whole time.

"She doesn't like jelly beans." He said the words quietly, his mind still working out her reaction to the candy and her statements about not liking sweets.

Something didn't click there.

A hand grabbed his arm, spinning him around. "Doesn't like jelly beans?" Suzanne's eyes widened, and her mouth dropped open. "Why the hell would they send her to us if she doesn't like jelly beans?"

Cal smirked, his turn to be the parent. "Suzanne, use your 'we are in public' voice, please. We don't want the neighbors, or heaven forbid, Holly, to hear you screaming about jelly beans." He grinned, planted a kiss on Suzanne's cheek, and strolled off whistling.

Holly was more than he'd expected. Pretty, smart, focused, and she did like his jelly beans. He'd meet her for breakfast tomorrow and plan the day with her. Later, he'd take her on the hike. He'd be smooth and cool, and she'd have a great time. It would be the best three-day visit ever.

Cal stubbed his toe on a crack in the sidewalk, bringing him down to earth. He'd never fix the split seam. It always told his wandering mind that he'd arrived home. He dashed up his walk, repeating over and over to set an alarm to visit the B&B first thing in the morning.

Chapter Seven

Holly woke with cotton mouth. Ugh, she hadn't even been drinking last night. And where the hell was she? She opened one eye and glanced around. Flowery wallpaper covered the space, from the nineties by the design of it. A floral comforter with several layers encased her like a sausage. The air did not contain the life-giving scent of coffee.

Then it hit her. She was in northern New York on a story, and she'd fallen asleep in her clothes. With a groan, she shoved off the heavy blanket and scanned for a coffee pot.

Nothing.

What kind of hotel room didn't have a coffee pot? Was it in the bathroom?

She slugged out of bed, yawning and stretching. Perhaps those alcohol-themed jelly beans from yesterday packed more of a punch than she suspected. Everything appeared too fuzzy to be normal. It was probably the lack of life-giving coffee in her system. She picked a door in the room at random and discovered a closet. She tried the other one and found the little hallway lined with more doors. She turned and scanned her room.

Where was the bathroom?

With a sigh, she grabbed her room key. Okay, the place was a cute, little, family-run bed-and-breakfast converted from a traditional home. The bathrooms were most likely communal. *Eww*, but what choice did she have at this point? Her editor booked the space for her, and he was clueless.

Tentatively, she tiptoed into the hall in her socks. She glanced up and down, but no obvious restrooms appeared to be present. Every door sported a number, and each stood firmly shut.

Crap, it must be downstairs.

The scent of burned toast hit Holly like a freight train. She had eaten nothing since the bad fast food. Her stomach growled as if a rabid wolverine wanted to escape. Carefully, she slid down the stairs toward what had to be the kitchen, forgetting her bladder in the process.

She wound around the bottom of the stairs through an adorable dining room, filled with ice cream parlor tables and frilly tablecloths. A solid door on swinging hinges stood at the rear, beckoning Holly. With silent steps, she made short work of the distance to it.

Within a couple steps of it, Holly halted as the door opened. A large dark-skinned man, dressed in a pink lacey apron, stepped out. Behind him, a cloud of smoke obscured the kitchen.

"Stay back," he said, his deep baritone streaked with trepidation. "You don't wanna go in there."

Holly clutched at her shirt, forgetting she hadn't brought her usual bathrobe breakfast attire. "Is there a fire?" she asked, skittering backward. If there were, they should evacuate and run for the hills. Because no way was she gonna die in a cute little B&B in a small town.

The door shut behind the man, and Holly recognized him, the night manager, Russ, who'd checked her in and showed her the room. A man of many talents, apparently. Smoke leaked under the door.

Except for a talent for cooking.

"No, not really. But the toaster..." He leaned over and coughed, a little wobbly on his feet.

Holly didn't think. She moved forward and supported him. She led him toward one of the bigger tables, one with chairs large enough to hold him. If she needed to carry him out of the fire, they were in trouble.

She plunked him into the seat and knelt at his feet. "Do you want some water? Should we call the fire department? Or an ambulance."

The man, his face a little ashen, shook his head. "Just... need... to catch..." he panted, rolling his wrist as he coughed. "Asthma... toaster... I..."

Holly patted his arm to stop him from talking. "Sit and breathe. I'll call someone..." She stood and glanced around. No phones in the dining room. Probably, there would be an old wall unit in the kitchen in such an old house.

Going to her room might not be a good idea if there were a fire. She lightly grasped Russ's arm. "Phone?"

The man, continuing to cough and huff, pointed to the front door.

The reception desk, of course.

Holly spied a pitcher of water on a breakfront and dashed over. She poured a glass, handed it to Russ, and hurried to the front desk. She searched, surprised the phone didn't sit right on top. Frantic frustration danced up Holly's spine. No phone, sick manager, and a fire. She spun in circle unable to do anything.

Then the Inn's main door opened, and Callum McIntyre strode inside.

"Morning," he said with a smile as casual as casual could be. He tilted his head, shining his grin over her and his red hair shone in the watery light. Holly was never so glad to see anyone.

Cal sniffed the air, his eyes widening. He dashed away toward the dining room before Holly spoke a word.

She stood, wide-eyed as he disappeared into the kitchen. Holly blinked, terrified that Cal would charge into a fire. She walked with stiff legs toward the kitchen door and cracked it open.

Cal stood next to a counter, a fire extinguisher pointed at a toaster. He fired off a couple of rounds of foam and stood back. He sniffed the air again, like a pointer dog, and rounded on the stove. He flicked off a burner and the oven, then turned to Holly.

"Breakfast will be delayed. Give this to Russ." He tossed something at Holly, and thanks to a dozen years of softball, she caught it easily.

In her hand sat an inhaler. She dashed out the door to Russ, the cook/night manager.

"Oh, thanks!" he said, taking a long pull on the device once she'd handed it over. After a few clear breaths, Russ asked, "Was that Cal running through here?"

"I think he put the toaster out and shut off the hot stuff." Holly glanced at the closed kitchen door, worry wracking her gut. Flames did not engulf the kitchen; merely a ton of smoke filled the room.

Holly caught herself. Relief and anxiety warred in her brain. No fire alarm ever sounded, not even a chirp. Her chest constricted. That must be a code violation, not to mention dangerous. She turned to Russ as Cal rejoined them.

Cal put a large plate on the table with an oven-mitted hand. "What was that supposed to be, Russ?" he asked with a chuckle.

"Breakfast." Russ sounded utterly defeated as a resounding alarm screeched through the air. "Great. Now the fire alarm goes off… I don't know how my aunt did it." He buried his face in his hands.

"No worries, man." Cal patted Russ on the back. "I'll have your kitchen cleared out in two shakes. Then breakfast on me at the diner." He spun and headed for the kitchen.

Holly glanced from the distraught Russ to the swinging door Cal had disappeared through. Her brow furrowed in confusion. Did she miss something?

Holly focused on the inn owner. "Russ?" she asked. "Can I get you anything? Do you want me to call an ambulance or the fire department?" Hopefully, the man was okay, but he seemed way too upset not to require medical attention.

Finally, he raised his head. "I'm sorry. I should've canceled your reservation, Ms. Lincoln."

Holly blinked at him in shock. His inn was the sole place to stay in town. She'd have to stay in one of the pricier Lake Placid hotels if the B&B closed. Her expense account for the assignment only stretched so far. If he sent her packing…

Russ folded her hands in his, engulfing them. Holly gulped when she realized how large the man was. His voice and touch were as gentle as a small child's as he flashed a sweet smile at her.

"I inherited the place a few months ago. My great aunt and uncle passed unexpectedly, and I've been trying to make a go of it. You're the first guest I've dared to book. I have no idea how to run the place, much less cook breakfast."

After releasing her hands, he dabbed at his eyes. "They loved this place. I want to do right by them, but I'm no hotelier. I'm an IT guy." He shook his head, his frown more than pathetic.

Holly wanted to wrap her arms around the big guy and tell him everything would be okay. And she was not a hugger.

Ever.

"You need an assistant."

Russ's face lit up.

She raised her hands, leaning away from him. She wasn't offering to do the job, merely suggesting a solution. "Not me. I have a job already."

Cal sauntered into the dining room. The man had impeccable timing. "Perhaps start with a chef. I bet we can find someone who'd cook breakfast for a few people." He grinned, and Holly knew Cal had already formed a solution for Russ's problem.

"Do you think so, Cal?" The man's voice sounded full of hope, as if Cal offered a lifeline rather than a work reference. Russ seemed to be in over his head.

"Yep." Cal wiped his hands together. "The kitchen is okay. The burned food is in the trash, and I cleaned the fire extinguisher residue. You'll have to get the smoke smell out and do a deep clean in there. Anyone else staying here?"

Holly was impressed by how calm Cal remained. Yesterday, he'd been bouncing off the wall the whole day. Today, no run-on sentences, no flighty behavior. He charged the problem and solved it.

Russ shook his head. "Only Ms. Lincoln. She's a trial run. Of course, I was stupid enough to let a reporter stay on my first try." He tapped his fist against his forehead. "Stupid, stupid."

"Now none of that, Russell. You have a good place here. Your aunt and uncle hit bumps in the road, too. No one's expecting perfect. Not on your first go. I mean, you've got the bed part right, didn't ya?" He glanced at Holly, probably hoping for confirmation.

She nodded, but her bladder twinged. She never hit the head. "Uh, yeah," she said without confidence. Her statement might not boost Russ's ego, but a toilet was more important at the moment. "Except the bathroom part. Where is it?"

Russ blinked at her. "What about the one in your room?" His eyes grew wide. "Each one has a bath. I put a reporter in the one spot…"

Holly cut him off. "Self-reprobation later, okay? I gotta pee."

Her sentence broke Cal's calmness. He burst into laughter with the level of energy she'd witnessed yesterday. "Over to the right there." He pointed. "We can't have any more accidents."

Holly stuck her tongue out at him as she dashed for the little door under the stairs.

Cal slipped his hand in Holly's as they strolled out of the inn. She shot him a curious look, but he ignored her. It felt like forever waiting for her to get dressed and prepped for breakfast, and no way he'd let her out of his sight again.

She appeared clean, fresh, and professional with only twenty minutes to get ready. Her stomach growled as they headed toward Main Street.

"Hungry?" he asked with a wink.

"Surprisingly, yes. Even with Russ's idea of breakfast. What's the story there?"

Cal raised an eyebrow at her and swung their hands. Russ probably told her a bit of his sob story while Cal played in the kitchen.

Not that Russ was a sobbing kinda guy, just overwhelmed. Cal understood the emotion all too well. He'd had Grandma right there with him as he took charge of the store. Not only was Russ grieving, but he also was walking on a new path.

But Cal knew the perfect person to help. Would he share with Holly? Probably. He had a hard time keeping his mouth shut.

"How much of our town's dirty laundry will be in your story?" he asked, crossing over to Main. "Russ is a good guy, and I'd hate for his new venture to be trashed in a magazine."

Holly pulled her hand away and glared at Cal. "You believe I'm here to trash your town? Really?" She crossed her arms over her chest. "I've got better things to do than search for scandals in a tiny northern town. You're lucky I'm here."

Her words stung like a dozen paper cuts, and Cal's mood plummeted. He'd stepped in it again.

Hadn't Suzanne warned him to watch himself with the reporter? He assumed everyone was a good, welcoming person, ready to be friends and hang out. Suzanne reminded him that not everyone wanted to be his buddy and not to assume everyone had good intentions.

Holly was there for a story. Everyone wanted it to be an interesting, cheery story about the great Bakersville township. What if Cal had already ruined it by behaving chaotically and highlighting a few bad things about the town?

He considered: Nadia and the soda cooler, Suzanne and the candy, Kinley and her attention seeking, Russ and his terrible breakfast. Cal needed to work harder to present her with the wonderful part of his town and even more fantastic candy. Now he needed the town to do what he did.

He blinked at Holly, realizing he'd never answered her question. "No, you're not here to poke fun at us. But we aren't showing you our best side." He scratched his chin. "Let's try the diner for breakfast. After, we'll go see the wonders in my town."

Holly rolled her eyes. "I'm here to write about you and your candy shop. That's it. Let's do the demo you promised. After, I want to ask a few people around town what they think of your store."

Cal swallowed hard. The article sounded super short. "Oh, I have to introduce you to my grandmother. She's got some great stories about the shop from its first day. Let's talk to her today."

Holly twitched her head toward the diner down the street. "Fine, but breakfast first."

The aura around Holly drew him in. He wanted to show her everything—the town, the shop, himself—to connect with her. Something he hadn't done with anyone new in a long time. And not because he never left Bakersville.

He'd dated but never met anyone with a presence like Holly's. She was pure confidence in a classy outfit, though today's was another pretty but colorless ensemble. Not that dating Holly was an option. The woman lived downstate. She probably would never have given him the time of day if she hadn't been forced to come here to interview him.

In the morning, he couldn't wait to see her, hence his early arrival at the B&B. In his mind, they'd have breakfast with Russ and plan the day. He'd had no idea about Russ's lack of cooking skills. The poor man seemed depressed. Cal would talk to Wendy about Russ and set a meeting if she was game. She needed to expand her universe as much as Russ needed help.

But Holly… His mind always snapped back to her since she'd walked through his door. Their initial emails and phone calls had been pleasant, but the second he laid eyes on her, he was done. Which sounded crazy because love at first sight wasn't a thing, right?

He'd enjoy her company and get her number to say hi after she left because she'd leave, eventually.

And he'd be alone again.

"You're kinda intense, aren't ya?" Holly asked the obvious question as she slid into the booth at the cutest 50s-style diner she'd seen in a while. Cal kept quiet once she demanded breakfast before the demonstration. She'd only known him for a day, but she could read people.

Cal was a perpetual motion machine, unless thinking. Then he became quiet. Today, he seemed very quiet. Not conducive to a good interview or getting to know each other better.

The attraction between them bloomed, but the idea of the man in constant motion had her imagining him in bed. But no details. She was too tired and in deep need of caffeine. She could attack from the rack if the situation required it, but considering the fire and stress of the morning… She wanted coffee and an egg dish with a pile of carbs—fuel at any rate.

"Intense?" Cal asked, fussing with his silverware. He rearranged his as if they sat at a formal dinner. When he reached for her fork, she pulled it away.

"Always on the go, always moving." She put her elbows on the table and her head in her hands, staring at him intently. "Do you ever slow down?"

Cal laughed, his hands flickering over the table as if he didn't know what to do with them.

Yeah, he was cute and into her. They might have a brief fling before she headed downstate. Nothing more serious than a night or two. He lived in the north-eastest north part of the state, far from where her ambitions led her.

Cal shrugged. "I keep busy. The store and…" He waved his hand, indicating the town or maybe the diner.

"How did you know to save Russ this morning?" Her instincts said the two didn't plan the morning's drama, but she needed to be sure.

Cal didn't have to do cartwheels for her to write a pleasant story. Her boss would take nothing less than a pink puff piece with all the candy dressing. Plus, the town seemed too small for a real scandal or intrigue. She gained nothing by trashing anyone, but it might be nice if something dramatic happened. Drama would get her off the local color page and into Section One.

An awkward silence fell between them. Holly never meant to call him out, but it seemed suspicious that he'd arrived in time to save the day.

Cal scratched his head. "I hoped you'd want to have breakfast together. That's all. I haven't seen the inn since Russ took over. He's been kinda busy."

Holly smirked, leaning back. "More like overwhelmed. I don't understand why he didn't mention that he didn't cook. I'd have asked for only the bed part." She laughed.

Cal paused a second before he laughed as well.

"Yeah, I do not know why he never told anyone about his struggle. We're not some kind of Cabot Cove always helping and, in each other's business, but a few of us would help him. I will now that I know." Cal shook his head. "We're not perfect, but we are a community. Well, some of us."

He grinned, and Holly guessed the man was naming names in his head. She'd ask him later who the meanies in the town were. If he attempted to pass the place off as a utopia, she'd call him on it.

She had no use for pure sunshine. Real people were not like that. They resembled the Nadia girl, difficult for no apparent reason, or Suzanne, his manager, super suspicious, or Russ, overwhelmed with life. She wanted a town of those types of people, not cardboard cutout Northern New Yorkers in cable-knit sweaters and jokes about the weather.

And of course, as if summoned, two men in cable-knit sweaters entered the diner. They looked similar in appearance–dark hair, a bit scruffy, and down-to-earth. They sidled up to Cal and Holly's table with twin expressions of enthusiasm.

"Today," one said.

"You'd better be going," the other added.

Cal waved a hand at them. "Holly, meet Bakersville's star mechanics, Sam and Bert. They run the garage as you enter town. The one with a dozen gas pumps." The three men burst into laughter—apparently, a town joke. Holly smiled, pretending to understand.

"Nice to meet you." She narrowed her gaze, sizing them up. Both held a trace of the middle-age spread.

They appeared to be similarly dressed without twining, but in the end, they didn't look too much alike. What was their story?

"You're coming with, right?" the first man, Sam, asked. He pointed at Holly. "We can always use fresh meat." He winked, and an odd sensation pulsed in her belly, a kind of "my uncle said a bad joke" impression.

Bert sighed. "What my husband is trying to say is you are more than welcome to join us for the short hike today. He will *not* be playing any stupid pranks on the trip."

Sam held up his hands in a pleading gesture. "What stupid pranks? I do not know what you're talking about." He said "about" with the cutest Canadian accent.

Bert patted his husband's shoulder. "Fake snake in the sleeping bag has kept Inge from joining us for over a year."

Sam huffed. "She has no sense of humor. But Cal here… Cal would love a snake in his sleeping bag." He winked again, and everyone's breath caught.

Cal took the flirting in stride. "Sam, you're married, and Bert can kick my butt. No snakes for me. Sorry, man, not my game."

Bert shoved Sam away from the table. "You can see he's entertaining a nice lady. Why must you flirt?"

Sam shrugged. "Jealousy?"

"Of me or him?" Holly asked, getting into the game. These two were a hoot.

"Yes," Sam said. "Now about hiking…"

Cal glanced at Holly, a pleading look in his eye. "It's a short one because June hurt her foot, but the spring air and the mountains are beautiful. Might add a bit of color to your article." He shrugged as if it wasn't important.

Holly read his face and body language like a book. Cal was dying to get her out into the woods.

Yuck.

She hated camping and all the outdoors crap, but it might expose more sides of the man. She sighed and hung her head. "Is it super short?"

Both Sam and Bert pumped their fists. Yeah, those two were made for each other. "Sunset hikes are the best. Don't worry. We have extra everything for you, flashlights, canteens, first-aid kits."

Holly blinked at him. "Why would I need a first-aid kit?" She glanced at Cal, whose face turned a cherry red.

"Because," Bert said. "If you are hiking with Cal,

you'll want it. He tends to… What word am I looking for?" He turned to his husband.

"Run ahead willy-nilly?" Sam suggested.

Bert nodded. "And not look where he's going."

"One time," Cal protested.

"Six times," Bert corrected. "Anyway, I want coffee before I finish June's Harley repairs. Let's go, baby." He tapped Sam on the shoulder, and the two moved to an empty booth.

Cal started in on a hiking story where he absolutely did not twist his knee or need twelve stitches when he fell down a sinkhole.

Holly listened with a light smile on her lips. She bet Cal had a thousand more. She could listen to them all.

The idea stopped her cold. Yes, she felt attracted to him and was considering a quickie before she left. Listening to a thousand stories might take years. She wasn't ready for that. Not before she had a life and a career. No redheaded lumberjack would distract her from her goals.

Luckily, before she could fall further down that rabbit hole, the waitress arrived. A young woman in a 50s-style uniform, her hair tucked in a little cap. She looked adorable. A personal choice, or did the owners ask his servers to resemble pin-up girls from an earlier era?

She automatically poured them coffee. “The usual, Cal?” she asked, her tone short and quick as if she didn’t have time for chitchat. A good crowd filled the place, and not every server talked your ear off.

“Sure,” Cal answered. “Phoebe, this is Holly Lincoln. She’s writing an article on the shop. I’m showing her around town today.”

Phoebe eyed Holly as if studying her. “Huh,” she said. After a beat of awkwardness, she asked, “What can I get you?”

Holly, who hadn’t looked at a menu, rattled off a complex omelet order right out of *When Harry Met Sally*.

Phoebe listened and said, “It’ll be right up.” She turned and walked away.

“She’s good. No notes.” Holly remarked as the girl disappeared behind the kitchen door.

“Oh, yeah. Phoebe’s got a mind like a steel trap. Nothing gets past her.”

Holly dumped two sugars into her coffee. She reflected on all the interesting spots around town and the people who lived and worked there. Why was a sharp, smart girl working as a waitress? Holly saw another story there.

She took a long sip of her coffee and marveled. It tasted good, almost premium Seattle coffee good. She glanced at Cal, who put on a stupid, shit-eating grin once more.

"That would be Tess with the coffee. That woman makes the best in town. Mel, the owner, will never let her leave because of the coffee."

"So, she's trapped here in a gothic romance?"

Cal scratched his head. "Definitely." They laughed, drinking their coffee in the quiet murmur of the diner.

After a few minutes, a large man exited the bathrooms on the side of the dining room. "Phoebe. It's doing the thing again." He appeared to be a little embarrassed, with flaming red cheeks, and a lot annoyed. Everyone in the diner caught their breath before their eyes turned to Cal.

Holly joined them, her eyebrows raised.

Cal tossed his napkin on the table. "I'll be right back." He stood and headed for the bathroom.

Holly glanced around, a question on her lips.

Phoebe returned and sank into Cal's vacated seat. "It's the toilet in the rear. The tank locks up and floods the entire room. Coincidentally, it's always when Darrell uses the bathroom. I have no idea what he's doing back there, and I don't want to know."

She folded her hands on the table and looked at Holly with an expectant air. Holly stared back, her mouth curled down, unsure what to think of this woman. Meanwhile her brain imagined Cal cleaning an overflowing toilet.

"It's water," Phoebe said with a bored tone. "Nothing gross. But Mel won't fix it. So, Cal patches it every once in a while. He's a good guy. Anyway…" She pressed her hands onto the table. "You're the reporter." A statement, not a question. "I have questions. Why are you here?"

A few syllables of laughter escaped Holly's lips. Phoebe was not only smart but direct. "To interview Cal about his store. A puff piece for the local color section of the magazine."

Phoebe reached out a hand, not quite touching Holly's. "No, seriously, why are you here? I read your bio and your writing. Your last article was about baby animals in the Ticonderoga area. Now you're doing crap pieces on a candy guy in northern New York. What's the deal?"

Holly sat speechless. What was the girl implying? Holly crossed her arms over her chest and returned her gaze. "What do you mean?" The sugar disappeared from her voice. She hated being questioned, especially by a woman she didn't know.

Phoebe threw herself against the seat. "What is your editor thinking? Do they read your work?" She sat up again, pointing an accusing finger at Holly. "You're fucking good, and they have you writing about puppies. Jesus!" She threw her hands in the air. "What hope is there for the rest of us?"

Holly softened. If a waitress from northern New York understood her worth, hope bloomed that she might land a spot in a bigger magazine, a paper, or even TV. "Thank you. I think." She fidgeted in her chair, unsure where to go from here.

"I mean, you have talent, and they seem to be ignoring you. I want out of this town like no one's business, but I'm not the writer you are. I have no credentials to speak of. How am I ever gonna get out if they are dumping someone like you in our town?"

"Well," Holly stuttered, not prepared for a "get out there and fight for what you want" lecture. "It's about hard work and…"

"It's about knowing people. I told Cal to kiss your ass. Be super nice to you and get you on his good side. If he makes a good impression and you give him a glowing review, maybe someone important will come here and help me get the hell out." She finished with a flourish.

Holly attempted to process the dozen thoughts ringing in her head. First, Bakersville had both Saranac Lake and Lake Placid to use for tourism. The town was the perfect picture of small-town life in New York with its little shops and weird locals. Second, did the chick expect Holly to give her a hand up?

Sure, she'd be willing to mentor the girl, but not if the woman continued to be rude. And last, the one that hurt the most: was Cal being nice for a good review? Did their connection exist, or was he playing her?

Holly said nothing while Phoebe stared daggers at her.

Behind them, the bathroom door opened. Everyone turned to watch Cal exit. He held his hands out, his shirt spotted with water. “Flood avoided.”

The entire place erupted in applause, throwing Holly further off. The town celebrated the man at every turn. Of course, he did save them from disaster. Again. She narrowed her gaze at him before turning the look on Phoebe. Did they stage these “disasters?”

Cal strolled to his seat, sloshing as he moved. Water soaked his shoes and the bottom of his pants. He glanced at his seat and flinched. “Mel has to fix the pipe. I can’t keep doing it. I’m running out of dry shoes.”

Holly’s nose wrinkled.

“Just water, I swear.” He grinned at her, and, for the first time, his smile failed to fill her head with sunshine. “If it was another issue,” he put his finger to the side of his nose, “I’d be out the door like a shot.” He tapped Phoebe on the shoulder. “Breakfast better be on the house.”

The waitress rose and stood toe-to-toe with Cal, but only came up to his collarbone. “Doesn’t she have an expense account?”

Cal shook his head. “I did ya a solid. You won’t have to close and wait for Mario. Do me a favor?” His charm held an edge as if he was done with the young lady. Perhaps he understood Phoebe threw him under the bus.

“Fine,” she said, “but you better leave a tip. I’ll be right back.”

Chapter Eight

Cal resumed his seat. He should duck out and change. Holly's green tinge and grim expression said the bathroom thing grossed her out. The mood at their table appeared sour.

"I can go change if…"

Holly waved him off. She studied him. "Does it happen often?" She crossed her arms over her chest, her mouth turning down in a frown. The usual expression someone sported after Phoebe talked to them. With the girl's ambition to bust out of Bakersville, she'd probably given Holly the third degree.

Cal adjusted in his seat. Yeah, he'd have to store

clothes here if the pipe kept leaking. “Uh. Look, you seem…”

She cut him off. “Two days, three incidents.” She counted them off on her fingers. “The cooler at the pizza place, the toaster at the inn, and the bathroom at the diner. Interesting.” She sipped her coffee, grimaced, and placed it in front of her.

Cal’s mind raced, which never ended well. A thousand thoughts rolled over each other, each ending with Holly’s dark expression. He’d screwed up, and he knew it. The trust they’d built yesterday and this morning vanished like the smoke in Russ’s kitchen.

Crap. So much for a good article that might lead to more business, not to mention a new friend.

“Holly. I…”

She held up a hand. “I’m here to write a cutsie article and make you look good.” She stood. “But I can’t eat after…” She waved at the bathroom. “With you…” She gestured at him and shook her head. She tossed a twenty on the table before walking out the door.

Holly's temper refused to settle. She turned out of the diner and picked a random direction. Why the hell did she believe the gig would differ from all the others? She arrived, she wrote, she left. Same as always. Cal was nothing special.

The flirting, the heat between them, could earn her good copy. She'd considered a one-night stand with the man, but part of her wanted there to be more. He was handsome, lively, and charming without being an ass.

Or so she'd assumed.

He might be playing her to enhance the article. Perhaps the town wanted him to inspire her to do a larger feature about the entire village and engineered these "accidents" to make Cal appear to be a small-town hero.

And she'd fallen for it.

So much for being a big-city girl with street smarts and sophistication. These local yokels had played her for a fool. Best to leave now with only a little egg on her face.

After half an hour, she found herself at the bed-and-breakfast with no idea how she'd gotten there.

Might as well pack.

She entered the building, relishing for a second the beautiful Victorian interior, miles of wallpaper, and wainscoting. The furniture—settees, lounging couches, and delicate tables—appeared to be genuine antiques. The place looked once removed from an English manor.

Russ did not fit. Was this a setup, too? She sighed and headed for her room, glad the smoky smell had dissipated. She'd hate for the rugs to be ruined by a stupid stunt.

The door to her room stood open, and Holly froze in her tracks.

Great, now thieves.

She pushed the door open, ready to kung-fu whoever dared to touch her property. The door creaked open, and Russ straightened from where he stood by the bed, adjusting the duvet cover.

Oh, he was cleaning the room.

Behind him, a part of the wall appeared to be open. Holly rushed over, ignoring Russ's greeting. The space behind the wall revealed a luxurious bath with a full-sized tub. She gawked at the bathroom, then at Russ.

"This was here the whole time?" she asked, touching the wallpapered door. She pulled it shut, and the panel disappeared into a perfectly matched wall.

"Yeah," Russ said, surprised. "Didn't I demo the secret door when you checked in?" He scrubbed the back of his neck. "Oh, my God. I didn't. You thought there wasn't a bathroom in your room." He sat heavily on the bed. "I'm a terrible host."

Laughter burst out of her at the ridiculous situation. She'd had a secret bathroom the entire time. Russ seemed incompetent at his job. And she couldn't see the real story for a puff piece. Their adventure couldn't get much worse. She fell on the bed next to Russ, giving him a playful shove.

The man stopped his pity party and joined in her laughter. "Do you have any idea how long it took me to find the door? I needed to pull out the blueprints from the renovation."

The two of them rolled with laughter that edged on hysteria.

"Oh my God, you are so bad at this." She punched Russ's arm. "Get a damn assistant, you fool. How do you expect to make any money with no food, no bathrooms, and no fire alarms?"

"You looking for a job?" Russ asked between puffs of laughter.

Holly recalled the man's asthma and worried for a second. She tipped him back to sitting and tried to calm them both.

"Breathe, mister. I'm not sure your phones will call 911."

Russ laughed harder. He met her gaze and probably read her concern. He fished in his pocket, producing the inhaler. After a few seconds, he calmed down enough to take a hit.

"Better?" she asked, her hand on his arm.

"Yeah. I didn't expect you back so soon. Breakfast at the diner can be an event."

"Oh, it was." Her hysterics calmed, and her disappointment returned. "The diner bathroom…"

"Again? Man, they should either close the room or pay to have it repaired. I bet Cal fixed it, again."

Holly blinked at Russ. "It happens often?"

"Yeah, that and the drinks machine at the pizza parlor. They count on Cal to fix their stuff. He can do little repairs, but it's not his job. The town just expects him to step up and help." Russ shook his head. "I felt terrible about this morning. I don't want to do that to him, too. But I totally did."

The information slowly processed in her head. The town called on Cal. He hadn't staged anything. Well, the townsfolk might have, but not him. Or…

"Sorry if I'm interrupting." Cal stood in the doorway. A sick feeling rolled over him, seeing Holly sitting on the bed with Russ.

Cal had screwed up with her for sure. He didn't blame her for walking out at the diner, but had he acted like enough of a jerk for her to hook up with Russ? He *was* a pretty great guy.

Holly jumped off the bed, her face flushing a little pink. "Cal." Her voice sounded strained. "What are you doing here?"

With a hint of chagrin, he held out the bag from the diner. "Breakfast. Third time's the charm?" His smile felt weak, and he sounded off. "I'll leave it in the dining room." He turned to go downstairs when a hand on his arm stopped him.

"You changed." Holly sounded surprised.

"Yeah, well, you weren't the only one grossed out by the diner's bathroom." He shrugged. Part of him wanted Holly to go to his place with him and hang out while he changed. Not that anything more would happen. All the flirting between them up until now was for naught. Her look of disgust at the diner haunted him.

He handed her the bag. "Do you still want a demo? Or we could …" He hung his head, unsure where to go.

"Cal, let's go eat and talk." She turned to Russ. "Is it okay if we eat outside food?"

Russ laughed. "I encourage it. I'll talk with Mel about a delivery for tomorrow morning." He stood. "I'll check your towels."

Holly giggled. "Remember? I didn't use them."

Russ bent over laughing way too hard at her comment. "I forgot. Oh, man." He glanced at the rumpled covers. "I'll fix it. You two go eat." He waved them off, chuckling.

Holly grasped Cal's arm as they strolled down the stairs. The stairwell had barely enough room for the two of them to walk abreast, but Cal never complained. Physical contact seemed natural between them. Cal hoped it would continue after her visit.

"Did I miss something?" he asked as they arranged their food. Hopefully, she wasn't grossed out anymore and wanted to eat.

"Russ needs to work on his hotelier skills. He's sweet, though, and needs a helping hand." She sat regally, the queen of every room she entered. "He forgot to show me the bath in my room."

Cal slapped his forehead. The secret door! His great aunt and uncle were so proud of the suite. "It's gorgeous." Cal nibbled on a piece of bacon. "I hope he's not charging you an arm and a leg. It's the best room."

Holly shrugged. "I have no idea. I'm the sole person here. I must be his guinea pig because he gave me a bottom-tier rate."

"Makes sense. He's been in town for about a month. He seemed determined to continue the B&B. The mayor begged him not to close. It's the only rooming house in town. We get a few tourists. With summer coming, I hope he can make a go of the place."

They turned into the dining room and pulled out a few chairs. They'd clean their mess after. One less thing for Russ to worry about. They pulled out the to-go containers and dove in.

Holly glanced around, her eyes distant. "He's got a job ahead of him. Maybe the local fix-it guy can help him out." She pursed her lips and cocked her head.

All the bricks fell into place. The stupid accidents of the last two days, and Cal being there to save the day. She probably assumed he'd planned everything.

"Holly, I didn't…"

She waved him off. "I know. Russ told me a bunch of the businesses count on you to help them. They expect you to do repairs for free, and you are too nice to say no." She smirked, waving her fork at him. "True?"

Cal scrubbed his neck. "True. I did those stupid odd jobs before I took over the shop. I did a little of everything. Yeah, I can't say no. I can fix stuff pretty fast, enough to let them limp through, like at the diner."

Holly shoved a bit of the eggs in her mouth, her eyes shining. She said nothing, and Cal felt compelled to fill the silence.

"It began as a small thing. I fixed the cooler and a couple of lawn mowers. Then bam! Everyone started calling me as if I were a handyman. But I had candy to create. Well, usually. I can finish my work by noon or so, then I work the counter. We were doing so well, and Wendy wanted more hours anyway. So, I took the liberty to…"

Holly put her hand over his. "I get it. Don't allow them to abuse you too much. Sounds like you do a lot for them."

He swirled his hash browns around the container. "They do for me, too. They buy candy by the bucketful. Easter, Halloween, Christmas, Valentine's Day. They come through with huge orders. It's all good." He smiled, realizing the truth in his statement. This was his town, his people, and he loved it here.

They ate in silence for a bit until the tension forced him to speak. He worried he'd lost her interest for good.

"So, uh. The store opens at nine. Usually, I have the candy finished by then. I figured making some jelly beans together would give you some insight into the shop. A demo for the article," he reminded her.

"Yeah, sure." She leaned low over her plate, conspiratorially. "But I don't like jelly beans."

Cal grinned. "You sure liked them yesterday." Holly blushed a bright red, and Cal felt a wave of hope.

They packed the breakfast trash, and Cal deposited it in the kitchen. The room didn't appear to be too smoke-damaged. He'd call Wendy today and ask if she'd cook for Russ. Yes, he did exactly what Holly reprimanded him for, but how could he not help Sonia and Peter's nephew? He jotted a note for Russ.

Call 555-5556 and ask for Wendy. Tell her you need a cook.

Cal smiled and returned to Holly, ready to knock her socks off with his own cooking skills.

Chapter Nine

Cal held out his elbow to escort Holly to his shop. With all the ridiculous distractions they'd encountered, he wondered if he'd be able to actually do the demonstration today. Nothing about Holly's visit had gone as planned—typical for him. But her?

Holly seemed more of a planner, and he hoped he hadn't thrown her off. Something about her struck a chord inside him. She was gruff, grumpy, and interesting. Not that other women in Bakersville weren't fun to hang with. But the reporter from the big city pushed his buttons.

He'd be teased mercilessly for giving her all his attention while she visited. He couldn't help himself. Controlling his impulses was not in his wheelhouse.

The two chatted amiably for a few minutes when Holly asked, "Are we going the right way?"

Cal glanced around and noticed they were headed in the wrong direction. Heat rose in his face at his absent-mindedness. But Holly had stolen his attention with her bright eyes and wide mouth and…

He scratched the back of his head. Yeah, they were about two blocks off. Oops. "Scenic route?" He grinned at her, took a left turn, and walked to the store.

"Uh, okay." She glanced around, blinking. "So this candy-making demonstration…" She tugged on the strap of her messenger bag.

"Yeah, I got it set up back at the store. Sorry about the detour. I was wandering, as I do sometimes. We can jump right in as soon as we get there." Holly's presence distracted him more than he'd realized. He'd need to double down on his focus to make it through the demo.

Aware that his face shone beet-red, he ignored the sensation and waved Holly into the kitchen. He needed to get a handle on this. Maybe his leaky thoughts resulted from the fluttering in his stomach every time she was near.

She placed her bag by the hooks in the back of the room, paused for a long second before choosing an apron. Her hand hovered over the plain white one. She glanced at him for a half second, then chose the baby blue. Finally, a little color. She tied the apron on expertly, at home already.

Already?

He had to stop thinking about her as more than a reporter. Holly was a city girl and wouldn't be moving to Bakersville anytime soon. Their few conversations told him her ambitions appeared to be greater than his cozy little town. Still, he enjoyed seeing her comfortable in his kitchen.

"Have a seat," he said, waving at the workstation stools. "I'll arrange a few things first." He wandered around the kitchen, grabbing bowls, molds, and ingredients, ignoring the setup he'd created this morning.

Holly appeared bored, hunkering in her chair, her expression distant. She might be hungry after the weird breakfast mess. With lightning speed, he created another tasting tray, but different from Suzanne's. Holly would be a perfect test subject for the mochi.

With a flourish, he placed several bonbon-shaped treats in front of Holly. "Give these a taste and tell me what you think."

"Another tasting? You know I don't have to sample one of everything in the store." She glanced down at the tray and scrunched her nose. "Still no chocolate?"

Cal laughed. "No, you know there won't be." He pushed the plate closer to her. "Just try one. I'm thinking of expanding this line." He plopped his elbows on the counter, his chin on his palms,

She gazed at him, leery. "What are they?"

He smiled and continued to watch her closely.

She fidgeted. "Do you always watch people eat?"

He laughed and spun away. His body language hit ten on the intensity level, and he knew it. Time to dial it back. "If I watch your reaction, I get an honest impression. If you tell me, you'll be too polite."

Her smirk lit her face. How did she do that? "I'm never polite."

"Excellent."

She nibbled on the edge of a piece.

"No. Pop the whole thing in your mouth. Get the total experience."

Her eyebrows raised, and her mouth turned down. "Fine," she grumbled and put the white mochi in her mouth. A slow smile crossed her lips. "Not bad. Oh, there's a strawberry inside. Nice. It's not chocolate, but I wouldn't say no if I found them in my holiday basket."

Cal grinned. "Fantastic."

Holly's frown and glum expression remained. Did the whole breakfast event throw her off him? Maybe she lost her excitement for writing about his shop. *Oh no.*

"Hey," he said, catching her eye. "What's wrong?"

She stared at the plate of mochi. She dragged one toward her. "I want more color for the piece. My boss wants a snapshot of the town." She paused, eating another mochi. "You'd be the center and the shop, but my editor implied…"

Cal's mind ran like a hamster on a wheel. "Well, you've seen the diner, our award-winning pizza shop, the general store, and the bed-and-breakfast. We could visit the antique shop and the garage. They restore cars, not just pump gas. Plus, we haven't hit the book shop yet." He tapped his chin. "And there's the mountains."

"Whoa," she held her hands up. "I need four or five elements. Not a dozen."

Cal sat in the seat next to her, resisting the urge to grab her hands. She didn't seem like a touchy-feely person, and he'd already invaded her personal space too much during her brief visit. That didn't stop him from wanting to hold her hand or grasp her arm, to connect.

"Okay, about that hike. In the spring, a group of us head out to Whiteface and check out the spring growth, help clear trails, and sometimes camp overnight if the weather holds."

"Yeah, no overnights. No, thank you."

"So, you won't go?" He didn't mean to fill the few words with such sorrow, but it seemed to affect Holly.

She sighed, throwing her hands up. "Fine. I'll go." She seemed to be working hard not to roll her eyes.

Cal jumped up from his chair and did a fist pump. Not the right reaction, but a nice hike in the beautiful spring air would reveal how amazing the Adirondacks were. She'd fall in love, he knew it.

"But not overnight. Eww."

And the sentence threw Cal back into the doom and gloom mood Holly was laying down. He sighed.

"Not overnight. It's still a bit cold," he hedged, trying to keep the disappointment out of his words. "Anyway, a demo." He shuffled to the cabinets, pulling out more ingredients at random.

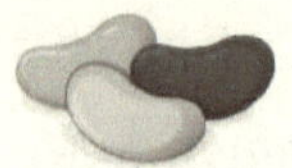

Holly bit her lip, watching Cal dance around the kitchen space like a pro. And he was a pro. She, on the other hand, burned water all the time. Her lifestyle comprised frozen dinners and takeout, and they planned to bake jelly beans? Did one bake them or boil them or… She had no idea.

She could have slapped herself on the forehead for her lack of research. Again. She researched a thousand topics last night, but not how to actually make jelly beans. She found sixteen thousand videos on the internet on how to do it. She never watched even one.

Cal buzzed around the kitchen gathering ingredients and cooking utensils.

Holly bit her thumbnail. Perhaps her lack of research gave her a fresh perspective. Knowing other chefs' techniques and ideas might have tainted her perspective. Coming in blind would add a novel element to her story.

Wow, even she couldn't navigate such a load of bullshit.

She'd failed to do her job. Maybe "ace reporter" lay beyond her skill set. She shook her head, tossing away the negative thoughts. She'd embrace the story, whatever it was, and put serious effort into this adventure.

She watched Cal, who talked a mile a minute as he prepped. His cute little apron covered his jeans, and his tight white T-shirt showed off his trim torso. Seeing a view like this one every day might not be too hard on the eyes. Lose the shirt and jeans. Leave the apron.

She grinned.

"What's your smile for?" Cal asked, pausing next to her. "It's the grin of someone who has a secret. Care to share?"

Holly shook her head, too embarrassed to say anything.

"Oh well," Cal shrugged. "As I was saying, it's all in the prep. If you have everything you need, you can go with the flow. You've got the apron. Go wash. Really well. Like really, really well."

He cocked his head to the side. “Having you mucking about in the store’s kitchen might put me in serious trouble with the health board. If you’re clean, covered, with your hair up, you’re good.” He shot a finger gun at her.

Holly slid off her stool, rolling her eyes. “I need a hair tie.” She reached for her purse.

“Or use this.” From under the counter, Cal produced a shower cap-shaped piece of plastic. He pulled the elastic and slingshot it at Holly. The plastic hit her in the face.

“Uh!” She stumbled backward, knocking her chair over. One didn’t expect a face slap in a cute little candy shop kitchen. Annoyingly, her apron came untied, and she almost tripped over the ends before righting herself.

“Oh shit, sorry.” Cal scrambled around the island and scooped up the hair cap. “You okay? I didn’t mean to…” His words trailed off as Holly flashed him the death stare.

She felt annoyed but not upset. She allowed Cal to take the lead too much. He seemed to pick a path and expect her to follow. Well, if she hated anything, it was following.

She snatched the cap from his hand and turned her back. She purposefully stood too close. Time to use her feminine wiles to knock him off kilter. It might even the score.

She stifled a laugh at her choice of words. Who even used the phrase "feminine wiles?" She needed to get in the right headspace for the article. Sex appeal was not the vibe she wanted. But she just couldn't help herself.

"Tie me," she said. Her words fell low and sexy.

"What?" Cal stepped away, but Holly followed him, her butt inches from the front of his apron.

"Tie me." She fluttered the strings of her apron behind her.

After a half-second pause, an "oh" escaped his lips. He grasped the sections of cloth and tied them together. The apron tightened around her middle.

When she was sure he had finished, she leaned against him. "Thanks. And for my hair…" She swept her mane up, exposing her neck, aware he hovered inches above her.

An audible gulp sounded behind her.

"Cal?"

"Yeah?" His question sounded breathless.

"Where's the cap?"

"Uh…" He sounded lost.

His response broke the lovely tension between them. The world settled beneath her. She enjoyed being in control, in charge. She'd allowed Cal to control the situation too much with his wonky ways.

She stepped away from him and plucked the cap from his hand. She pulled it over her hair, aware of how goofy her expensive cut would appear trapped under plastic. It was fun to tease. "Where's yours?"

Cal, who stared at her slack-jawed and wide-eyed, held up a second cap, rumpled and crushed.

Holly grinned. "How does one make jelly beans?"

His mouth snapped shut, and his eyes gleamed. "Let me show you."

Cal rubbed his hands together. The demo would either make or break the article, and whatever was brewing between him and Holly as well. He never planned to share his secret recipes or his complicated process, but he needed to let the woman in a bit. And with the way she was flirting… Anyway…

He was ready. He'd prepped everything beforehand, and the demo could not go wrong. He'd made jelly beans thousands of times over the years. Today was no different, well, except he planned to do a quick version. He'd be performing for an audience—that was all—an audience who would tell the world, or at least New York, about his beans.

He gulped. The idea of the whole world knowing about him suddenly made him feel very exposed. He glanced around the room, realizing that whatever Holly said about him would be read by hundreds of people, or thousands, or even millions.

"Where do we start?" Holly's gaze flitted around the room, drinking everything in.

Had he cleaned enough? Was it organized and ready to go? Panic crept into his soul, which was not good. A stressed Cal became a talkative, out-of-control Cal. Holly's games with the apron threw him off, but seeing his worktable set with his tools, he calmed.

He licked his lips, pulled in a breath, and began.

"Since it's your first time making beans, we'll keep it simple and choose the flavor first." He waved a hand over the counter where he'd placed various flavor oils and juices.

"What are these?" Holly strolled over and picked up a bottle. "Pineapple? Mint? How do you choose?"

Cal waited, and she moved on.

"Juice?" She raised the bottle of apple juice. "Is that how you put the flavor in there, or is it these guys?" She wiggled the extract bottle in the air, weighing it against the juice container.

"Choose what flavors you want. You can always use plain water and add more sugar if you don't use juice. I do them both ways."

Holly leaned over the counter, an enigmatic smile on her lips. "So, you do go both ways. I'm telling Sam."

Cal didn't fall for her joke. "Sam knows I use juice. I'd never hide it from him."

Holly knocked him in the ribs, and they both fell to laughing.

"Apple juice is a good base, and you can use it for a variety of flavors. It changes the taste a little, but with the right combo, it's fantastic."

Holly tapped the bottles, considering. “So, not the mint?” she asked.

Cal shook his head. “No, mint is a water-base usually, but we can try some interesting combos if you want. We’re making a mini batch so we can be silly.”

Holly turned away, as if making another little joke. Her flirting was contagious and he loved it.

Finally, she tried to throw her hair back and giggled when she failed. The net allowed no hair tossing. “Flavor choice, check.” She held up the apple flavoring and juice. “How long will it take?”

“Overnight at least, if we want them to be sellable for the store. I have to cook the sugar, then let them harden. After, the gels absorb the sugar. If I want them fancy, I have to tumble them with a little wax to make them shine.”

Holly put the bottles on the counter with a clatter. “That long? You can’t whip up a batch for lunch.”

Cal shrugged. “There are ways to get ’em done quick. You can toss the molds in the freezer, for example. I only do it for certain types. I can cook it in various ways and end up with tons of variants on the beans. It depends on what you’re looking for.”

Their gazes met, and Cal experienced that pull again. Unsure if it came from her boldness, her seriousness, or her ability to tolerate his ADHD, he felt the connection even though they'd met only twenty-four hours ago.

He stepped closer as if he planned to grab the juice and flavoring. When he stood next to her, he asked, "What *are* you looking for?"

Holly blinked at him, her brown eyes wide, a twinkle of desire in her gaze. "Something that might take a while. No quickies here." She put a hand over her mouth. "You know what I mean." But her pink cheeks betrayed her.

It seemed as if she was into him as much as he was into her. With this level of heat between them, he might convince her to stay in town for a few more days. They'd cement things and make a plan. Long-distance relationships worked all the time. With Suzanne and Wendy to cover for him, he could see Holly on weekends and…

"It sets up overnight?" Holly refocused on the beans.

Cal pushed the intrusive thoughts away. A platonic relationship would make things easier in the long run.

Besides, they were in the shop, and Suzanne might bust in any second.

He stepped to the side, breaking the intimacy. “Yes, and then some. Days.”

“That long?” Holly’s eyes bulged out of her head.

Cal snickered. “If you do it right, it can take even longer.” He clapped his hands together. “Anyway, we’ll start the flavor process and put the pots on the boil.” He turned away, wanting to take the woman in his arms, aware that such a bold move would be frowned upon. His hyper mind flew with a thousand scenarios, but his body remained on autopilot. He could create jelly beans in his sleep.

He busied himself by placing a large pot on the stove top with water, sugar, gelatin, and juice. He assigned Holly the task of mixing the coloring and flavor.

“We add it in? Aren’t jelly beans clear in the middle?”

“It’s one way to do it. Make a clear gelatin center and add the flavor as part of the shell. It takes longer. We’re going to infuse the flavor inside. I do that for most of my jellies. That way, I can taste it before it’s complete and see if my mixtures worked.”

"Like the whiskey ones?"

Cal nodded. "It took me a bit to figure out how to add the 'sparkle.'" He checked the pot and wished it would hurry up.

"You're not going to tell me the secret of the whiskey beans, are you?" Holly stirred the sugar on the stove as Cal directed. *What a pain to constantly stir the liquid.* She'd be bored with such a job in three minutes.

But Cal seemed to thrive. He'd check in on her progress with the sugar and then hop around the room gathering items, mixing ingredients.

On the counter, he'd deposited a couple of molds, large spoons, and a candy thermometer. Holly turned to examine the items, but Cal slithered to her side. He stood behind her, way too close, and she loved it.

The guy radiated sex and fun. She needed some serious fun in her life. He practically wrapped his arms around her as he corrected her stirring.

"Okay, see those little crystals forming on the side." He produced a small paintbrush from somewhere.

A paintbrush?

The number of tools for the project baffled her. Weren't jelly beans supposed to be simple?

He ran the brush around the inside edge of the pot, the crystals disappearing as he went. "You can't let those guys form on the pan. They'll burrow into the jelly and make the pot a bitch to clean." He leaned in further, his body aligned with hers at every inch. "Wanna try?"

Of course she did. She wanted to turn around and…

He placed the brush in her hand, gripped it, and guided her in a smooth motion around the perimeter. "I dip the brush in water first. If it sticks, we just redip."

Holly's nerves tingled with excitement, and her base brain urged her into inappropriate behavior. She spun around. Cal stood inches from her. Every impulse in her body said flirt.

"Redip? Is that technical jargon?"

The side of his mouth quirked up. "An industry term."

They were close, and he moved closer. "I could share more secrets, but…"

Heat soared over Holly, back to front. Her heart raced, and her blood surged. It would be a fantastic first kiss.

Cal's eyes widened. In a graceful move, he wrapped his arms around her and spun her away from the stove. Her head swam, and her feet scrambled for purchase beneath her.

He held her in his arms, her body slack as if he dipped her while dancing.

Redip…

"Whoa." He studied her. "You okay? Not singed."

Holly furrowed her brow. "What?"

Cal laughed, trying to put her on her feet. "The stove, the pot. You were practically in the flames. One fire is enough for today."

Embarrassment flooded her. That's why her backside felt hot. With the warmth between them, she'd forgotten about the actual heat behind her.

"I'm fine." She glanced away, her face blazing.

Cal tipped her chin to face him. His smile appeared warm and sweet. Those cornflower-blue eyes scanned her over, and her stomach clenched. Maybe they'd have that first kiss after all.

"You look fine to me." He brushed his lips over hers, the gentlest of touches, the sweetest of gestures. And the world stopped. The heat of his body and the touch of his lips on hers spun her head in spiraling circles. It was the sweetest, purest kiss ever.

And Holly was gone.

Her legs wobbled as he pulled away, and she reached out for the counter to steady herself.

What just happened?

His frantic, energetic manner disappeared. His focus seemed to be completely on her for a beat. They stood silent for a second, processing the kiss.

Cal broke the mood. He sniffed the air and frowned. "Have a seat for a bit. Let me fix it."

The candy!

She'd stopped stirring, and the batch might be spoiled. She regretted ruining the candy, but that kiss… Her mind and heart whirled. Cal was not her usual type. She preferred a sleek, sophisticated city guy. A small town man in an apron made a refreshing change.

Dreamily, she wandered over to the stool and plunked down. "I ruined it, huh?" She didn't want to return to business, but she needed the material for the article.

"Nah," he said. "It's fine. We'll toss it in the freezer to cool for a bit. I usually let it sit out and cool in the air for a few hours. Fewer ice crystals that way, too."

He removed the boiling pot from the stove and transferred the liquid to three bowls. He was well-organized. He maneuvered everything to the fridge, balancing the three bowls with ease.

His body moved gracefully around the space. He pulled another container from the fridge, brought it to the counter, and placed it next to a stack of molds.

"So, with the long downtime for the beans, I prepped ahead." He placed the bowl on the counter.

Holly focused on it, though no longer interested in making jelly beans. She wanted another of those little kisses and a bit of quiet time with the cook.

He'd never appeared as calm and collected as when he cooked. Usually, his energy tired her out. But currently, he was an amiable companion. Not that she didn't enjoy his hyper moments, but the kiss…

She sighed.

"I lost you, huh?"

She met his gaze, sure her lack of enthusiasm shone on her face. "You could tell?"

He chucked, placing the bowl down and grabbing a spoon. "ADHD here. My brain gets super focused one minute and completely disinterested the next. Distractions are…" He wiggled his eyebrows. "Distracting."

Holly laughed. "I'm sorry, I …"

Cal shook his head. "I kissed you. Mea culpa." Deftly, he spooned the sugar/gelatin mixture and deposited the perfect amount in each space of the mold. "The trick is not to over-pour. You want the beans to have the right shape." He continued filling the spaces. "Sometimes I create my own molds if I want different shapes or sizes."

Holly watched fascinated. He moved quickly and consistently. But he'd done this every day of his adult life.

"Does it get boring?"

"Making molds?"

She laughed. Cal wasn't a mind reader. In fact, he seemed pretty straight-laced. "No, the repetitious activity." She waved a hand at the second mold as he filled it.

Cal shrugged. "It's good for me. Grandma used this kind of chore to keep me busy. Repetitive activities are good for my brain. If my hands are busy doing something, my mind calms down. It's as if I understand I have a task to do and can focus on the one activity."

He swirled the mold around to level out the contents. "But it has to be a finite thing. I can't do large repetitive tasks. I can get lost in those. Short, focused activities work best."

Their gazes met again, and Holly's entire body thrummed at the idea of a focused activity with Cal.

He licked his lips and turned his head away. Okay, it might be mutual, but she planned to stay for another night or two. He was not a one-night stand guy. He seemed like a guy you'd spend months dreaming over. A man she could get used to, until they both realized their careers took them to different places.

If so, she needed to at least dig out the entire story on his allergy. A candy shop with no chocolate could be a great hook for the story, but to publish, she needed the details.

"So, you never told me what happened with your chocolate allergy. I need more meat for my story."

Cal paled and swallowed hard. "Uh, I…" He tucked his head down and fiddled with the molds, on the edge of spilling them. He glanced at her, and the pain in his expression struck Holly to the core.

He sat.

She stood.

Cal blinked, his head full of fuzz, his heart beating rapidly. He didn't want to tell the story. He would if it helped the article and made the chocolate thing a non-issue. Because she said yesterday it was weird, and he hoped she didn't think he was weird.

A hand touched his back, and a glass of water appeared in front of him.

"Do you need anything else?" she asked, swinging onto another stool. "You went vampire-pale there. Do you want an antacid or some sugar? Are you diabetic?"

He chuckled, feeling a little better. He sipped the

water, not too cold, not too warm. Perfect for a sour stomach.

"Diabetic? That'd be more ironic, huh? Chocolate allergies and diabetes? No, and I'm not lactose intolerant either." He raised the water before taking another sip. "Thanks for that. I get going and end up on a bad road before I'm aware. If I talk about certain things, I get upset."

She placed a hand over his, and his words stopped flowing. He stared at her hand, the warmth of her touch running up his arm. He'd grabbed her hand and dragged her around half a dozen times since he'd met her. She'd never initiated skin-to-skin contact before.

A warm smile snaked over his lips.

"Sorry. My brain… Yeah, so um… Grandma used to do the whole chocolate thing. My dad helped her and was ready to be her partner at one point. I was little when I snuck my first chocolate piggie. I was old enough to remember how delicious it was and how my throat tingled.

"I had a hard time breathing, and the grownups didn't see it. I smashed a china plate on the floor.

Grandma turned on me for a whooping and realized I was struggling.

"I don't recall much afterward. I woke up in the hospital with Grandma at my side. She promised no more chocolate. I felt okay with it. I still am."

Tears threatened his entire speech, and he almost made it—almost told the entire story in one breath. In the end, tears leaked down his cheeks, and he stopped talking. He'd tell Holly everything if he had to, but not today. He hoped for the piece to sound upbeat, not be the tragic story of a boy who came a hair's breadth from losing his life over chocolate. A boy who lost his parents because he snuck a candy from his grandma.

Holly watched the river of emotions flow over Cal's face. Sorrow, shame, anger…but only a little anger. She opened her mouth to say something, but Cal beat her to it.

"So," Cal said, lifting two molds and heading to the walk-in fridge. "The hiking trip…"

Clearly, he done talking about his allergy. *Oh, well.*

Holly laughed as she jumped up to open the fridge door for him. "Just like the pizza. Non sequitur much?" she asked.

He slid the molds into a section with small, tight shelves perfect for the trays. "Well, I mentioned it before, and you didn't answer. It'll be fun, and I promised June I'd go. She wants to meet you."

Holly considered. Hiking was not her thing. Cal kept bringing up this June woman without real context. She felt confused. "Is that your grandmother? I'm supposed to meet her, too."

"June runs the antique shop out on East Street. She's the one with the Harley. She has designs for turning our little Penny Saver into something more. She wants to pick your brain. No, she's not my grandma. She's everyone's aunt, though. She'll take you in in a second and make you her own. She's all gruff grumpus and teddy bear at the same time." He chuckled. "It's an hour of scenic trails here in the northern Adirondacks. How can you say no?"

She held a thousand excuses at the ready, but one look into those blue eyes, and she understood she'd be on the trail.

Chapter Ten

Cal practically did a victory dance. All thoughts of his origin story vanished from his brain. The tour of the town and the shop were nice and all, but showing her Whiteface and the wonderful scenic area surrounding his beautiful town was another thing. He'd be sure to bring his camera to take a snap of her expression when she saw the view from the ridge. He couldn't wait to take her.

They arranged to meet at the B&B in a few hours. The rest of the group planned for a later start, it being a weeknight, and the sun set later each day with spring's arrival.

Holly claimed she wanted to change her clothes. She mumbled about cute hiking boots as if a quick walk in the woods required the right wardrobe. She already looked adorable.

He'd packed a kit for both of them, hoping she'd say yes, eventually. He planned to go no matter what. He needed a good trek in the wild to clear his head. Even a short, easy one would do.

June always coerced them into trying out alternative paths, new trails. Usually, they ended up on the same ten-mile stretch on Whiteface or Mount Baker Peak. Not that he minded, but he'd love to head south sometime and visit the other peaks in the Adirondacks. June loved her home territory, though.

Sitting on the four-poster bed, Holly ran her fingers through her hair. A thousand competing emotions raced through her heart. Her mind refused to engage and make sense of situation. Cal McIntyre was a dangerous man.

Time to scrap the assignment and go home? Her editor would be disappointed, but she had a basic story to give him. Nothing stellar, nothing spectacular in her portfolio to grab a job at an Albany news channel, but at least for today, some copy. The town and especially a certain confectioner set her mind whirling. She couldn't discern up from down.

She bit her nail, unwillingly drawing a picture of Cal in her head: his red hair, his muscles, his amazing smile. A man was adorable but unrealistic for a relationship. He seemed cemented here in Bakersville. And Holly, well, she wanted something more.

Her phone jingled, snapping her out of her head. One glance at the caller ID caused her to groan aloud.

"Hello, Mother."

"Holly, that's not how you answer a phone." Her mother's shrill voice echoed over the line, and Holly cringed. She knew better than to mess with the woman.

"I'm sorry, Mother. I've had a long day. Thank you for calling me." It was best to drop to one knee and be respectful. Hortense Lincoln could eviscerate over the phone as easily as in person. Having a defense lawyer for a mom never made Holly's life any easier.

“Much better, my sweet. How is your trip? Staying away from the sugary junk at the store you’re covering? I can’t believe they sent you to Plattsburg to eat candy.”

Holly pressed her lips, aware the conversation was a test, as was any discussion with her mother. They never chatted; they squared off. Best to be subtle.

“The article is not only about the shop or the owner, who is quite a character. It’s about the entire town, Mother. Bakersville is considerably quaint.”

“Well, no story about a little town at the far end of the state will earn you the career you deserve. You’ve worked too hard and too long to end up writing frilly pieces about cotton candy.”

Holly could hear her mother’s eyeroll. “It’s not so bad, Mom.” She bit her lip again, recalling the hijinks of the trip so far—the fire, the running all over town, but then again, there was the pizza and some amazing candy.

“I could merit a multi-issue feature for the magazine. The town has several spots I can highlight for tourism. The editor is on board with at least a three-page spread for the candy shop and possibly more.” Her words faded off as the silence on the other end deepened.

"Holly, we did not send you to NYU to cover chocolate tastings…"

Holly broke into her mother's rebuke. "Actually…"

"Actually, nothing. I'm tired of watching you fail. You have an amazing education and opportunities throughout the state, despite that, you plunk away at that little magazine writing about dog shows. Is this what a NYU education merits?"

Tears burned in the back of Holly's eyes. They repeated the same conversation every couple of months. "When will you get a real journalism job?" or "I read your article. You can do better," and Holly's favorite "What new places have you applied to, and who can I contact for you?"

Holly was tired of pushing away her mother's coattails. Yes, the woman knew everyone in the state. She talked to reporters from the TV stations and real papers every day. Holly was not Hortense, and she never would be. She wanted to earn her place on a news team on her own. Her mother didn't understand.

Holly straightened her shoulders and swallowed. One more performance for the woman, faking confidence and poise. "The story has a great angle as the shop doesn't sell chocolate. There's a deeper story here, and I'm digging hard. With the right spin, my editor can sell the story to a larger venue. Possibly earn us a feature on the local news and beyond, perhaps in Burlington and Buffalo. I might record the story myself rather than have another reporter read my copy."

Holly heard tapping on the other end of the line, probably Mother tapping her manicured nails on the phone case. "Don't you dare allow another reporter to steal your story. I'll call Jim at Channel 9 and set up some things. Send me a summary so I can pitch it."

Holly repressed a sigh. "Mother, the Adirondack Chronicles assigned the story to me. I will need permission from Milton to send copy to other news agencies. He and I have a plan to distribute the article." Her mind raced, and she blurted out, "I can score a column from the town. The tourism interest alone would give me bank for the six articles I have for the town."

She closed her eyes, embarrassed by her arrogant lies. The conversations with her mother always ended up in a pissing contest, but usually, Holly didn't have to outright lie to her mother to put her in check. Holly wasn't allowed to arrange meetings with other news agencies about her magazine articles. Only her editor could do that. She could apply for jobs with her finished stories, but her mother failed to see how the system worked.

Hortense huffed. “I’m disappointed in you. Obviously, your little town there has a gold mine, and you’ll allow Adirondack Chronicles to have the entire story.” She paused. “Really, Holly, how do you expect to move forward to a proper job if you keep letting opportunities pass you by?”

Tension crawled over the phone lines. She should never have answered the phone or told her mother about the trip. Holly knew better. Nothing she did was ever good enough for her mother. She should’ve waited until the story was published before telling her mother, but who else did she have to tell about her life?

She scrubbed her neck and closed her eyes. “Milton and I would like to syndicate the articles. After they go around the state, since it’s New York tourism, I plan to contact the Albany, Buffalo, and Burlington news agencies. I’ll present my amazing feature and be hired by summer.”

Hortense snorted. "By summer? I hope so. Get moving, my beautiful child. Opportunity waits for no one. Go write your articles and send me a copy. I want to say I read your Pulitzer Prize work before the rest of the world."

"Sure, Mom. I'm on it." Without another word, Holly ended the call. Her mother pushed and prodded Holly to do more, work harder, to be more. She loved the woman for it. But sometimes, she pushed too hard or did too much for Holly. No one wanted a snowplow mom, and at her age. Holly should do everything for herself.

But she didn't. Not by a long shot.

She tapped her pen on her notepad. Would she write a stellar article or six on Bakersville and catch the attention of the networks? She hoped so, but in her heart, she doubted it. There had to be a way to get herself into a correspondent position from her current one. Without mommy helping, Holly had no clue how to do it.

Cal met Holly at the B&B and waved to Russ as he motioned her to the car. They'd have to drive to the trailhead to meet the group. Someday, he'd ask Russ to join in. But not now. The man appeared to be overwhelmed with the inn.

He loved how Russ watched over Holly before he arrived. Not that Bakersville could be dangerous or had undesirable characters, but witnessing someone being gentlemanly made his heart swell. Hopefully, the inn owner had no other intentions about Holly.

She kissed Cal after all.

She slid into the car and snapped her seat belt. "It's kinda late for a hike, isn't it?"

"Nah, we'll make a fire and roast some dogs for dinner. June usually times everything perfectly. We'll see the sunset on the mountain. Everyone has night equipment. Well, now we do. We got caught in the dark one time when we lost a trail marker. We always bring flashlights, headlamps, and such."

"I don't have any supplies. I have crappy sneakers and a jacket." She waggled a finger at him. "You better have sufficient equipment for both of us."

He waved at the two bags in the back seat. "I've got you covered. No worries."

She scoffed. "'No worries.' Seriously? Isn't everything going to be soaked? Isn't the winter thaw dangerous? It's been raining here for a week." She crossed her arms and focused her gaze out the windshield.

Not an outdoorsy person.

"Yeah, we have occasional flooding with the thaw, but this year hasn't been bad. The snowpack is melting as it should. Slow and steady. No flash floods."

"Great. You've jinxed us." She never met his gaze, and her mouth turned down in a fixed frown.

"You don't have to go, Holly. I wanted you to see more than the town. We've got so much going on here. I love living in the area. You're a city girl, but the mountains and rivers in the area are beautiful. I can drop you off if…"

He didn't add that he wanted to spend every moment with her, show her his home, and entice her to come back and visit often.

Holly sighed. "It's fine. I don't enjoy surprises. I never planned to hike, and the entire trip has been…"

He glanced at her and noticed her lips were pressed together. The puzzle piece fell into place. "Oh," he said and kept his gaze forward. She didn't like him after all. He was too chaotic for her. It was her way of telling him. "I see. I'm…"

"That came out wrong, Cal." She reached for his hand. "I mean…"

"It's okay. I can be a bit much. I don't plan well. I let Suzanne and Grandma plan stuff for the store. I go with the flow. I'm sorry if I threw you out of your comfort zone. You don't have to go." He pulled over to the side of the road, ready to bang a uey.

"No, Cal. It's fine. I'd like to meet your hiking group and see the mountains. It will add some great color to the piece. I can be flexible. I'm…"

Her words trailed off, and Cal didn't know how to answer. Was the heat between them in the kitchen merely the stove, and the flirting only a light banter, nothing more? He'd kissed her, a little thing, but she seemed fine with it. Maybe downstate people smooched all the time.

He drove on in silence, a fool for hoping a sophisticated city woman would see anything special in his chaotic world.

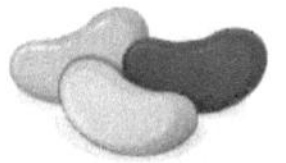

Holly chided herself for saying such mean things to Cal. She felt exhausted. She'd hardly eaten the whole trip. Last night's sleep seemed like a blip.

The cooking activity threw her for a loop. Her mind spun over what had happened there. She had no plans to fall for a small-town guy who stood firmly rooted in a little Podunk tourist town.

She refused to fall, so her brain said, but her heart…

The entire experience in Bakersville consisted of shock after shock after shock. She wanted some downtime. Hopefully, the hike would prove to be a tranquil activity.

She could chat with the other members of the group if being with Cal became too much. Too much activity, energy, and heat between them. She'd encouraged him too much, allowed him to kiss her, loved their sweet kiss… It lingered in her mind, taking up way too much space.

Focus woman. You have a job to do.

But could she really do it anymore? Could she be unbiased about the sweetest, funniest man she'd met in a long time? A man who made her question her goals and convictions.

They'd hike and return to separate beds. She'd interview the grandmother, write the piece, and go home. It'd be over in a few days. Her life goals did not include a cute candy maker.

Cal parked the car at a lot by the side of the road. A trail head peeked out from the new green foliage emerging from the trees. It was gorgeous already.

Seven people stood by the entrance near a large wooden sign. A woman with short gray curly hair directed the group. As Holly exited the car and accepted the pack from Cal, she noticed the woman wore a walking cast on one foot.

"Can she do the hike with a cast?" Holly whispered to Cal

"Of course I can," the woman boomed. "I wouldn't be here if I hurt. If I want a breather, I'll take it." She raised her chin and met Holly's gaze. A fierce determination glinted in her eyes. Everything about the woman, from her short gray hair to her stocky frame, said she must be June.

"Hey, everyone!" Cal waved his hands to catch their attention. "This is Holly Lincoln with *Adirondack Chronicles Magazine*. She's doing the article on my shop and chose to join us today." He returned June's glaring gaze. "So, be kind."

Introductions were given all around. Surprisingly, Holly had met the entire group in their adventures around town. Sam and Bert were there. Apparently, Asa from the pizza shop and Kinley from the general store were avid hikers. All in all, it seemed like a pleasant group.

"All right." June clapped her hands to bring the focus to herself. "We are doing Trail C, no variations. We'll stick together in twos and threes. We'll meet back here no later than eight pm. If you are not here by eight, we call the rescue squad. Questions?" She put her hands on her hips and dared anyone to question her.

"Eight?" Sam asked. "Do we need that much time? I mean, honestly, we are all experienced hikers, and C is the easiest." They appeared disappointed in the chosen path and meeting time.

June sighed as if a great burden had been placed upon her. “Sam. I’ve got a bum foot, Cal’s got a newbie with him, and it’s spring. Tell me half of you won’t stop every two seconds to snap a nature pic. Things are blooming everywhere. Tonight is a nice, quiet walk. Next week, we hit Whiteface for the ten-mile trail.” She grinned.

Asa raised his hand. “Are you sure you’ll be up to it? I mean…”

June cut him off with a glare. “It doesn’t matter. You’re going, even if I can’t.” She threw her arms out. “You aren’t getting the club thing, are ya? We go together for support, but if one person can’t come…”

“Well,” Cal interjected. “You *are* our leader, and we do look to you for guidance.” He fluttered his eyelashes.

She jabbed a finger at him. “You cut it out, mister. We’re a club, not a monarchy. Anyway…” She waved off further comment and barked out, “Flashlight check.”

Everyone in the group produced a light source in some shape or form. Cal handed Holly one resembling a baby spotlight.

“Really?” she mouthed.

He shrugged, raising his own version. These people took their flashlights seriously.

"Whistles?" June asked. Again, each person produced a sound device, most on chains or lanyards around their neck. Cal handed one of these over to Holly.

"Safety first," she said, putting it around her neck.

"Oh, no. Food first," Bert said and held an insulated bag. "We'll head to Rest Stop Six and grill some dogs. Who's packing?" He looked around the group with a huge grin.

Asa tapped his bag. "I have macaroni salad, one vegan, one full of tuna."

Kinley tapped her backpack. "Apples, grapes, and a tangerine or two."

Cal produced a bag from his pack with a flourish. "Super Sour Suckers!"

Half the group groaned, half cheered.

"Got anything else?" Bert asked.

Cal huffed, stowing the sweet treats away in his pack. "These were specifically requested, I'll have you know."

"Yes, they were!" Sam nudged his husband, a huge grin on his face.

"Yeah, but you always have a ton of candy in your bag. What else did you bring?" Asa asked, a hopeful glint in his eye.

Cal opened his mouth to speak, but June cut him off.

"Some of us are doing these hikes for exercise and health. Not to walk the trail eating candy. No offense, Cal."

"None taken."

Holly plodded along behind the group, trying to keep up with Cal. At last, the path settled into a super cute rest-stop-overlook spot. Picnic tables and port-o-potties were blessedly absent from the scene. A large fire pit surrounded by logs sat in the center of the clearing.

Sam produced a small rack from his bag and had the hot dogs on the fire in minutes. The picnic atmosphere felt light and fun, though the clouds began to stack on the side of the mountain.

June rallied the troops after half an hour. She pounded home the cleanup, ensuring they left no trash behind.

Kinley kept peering at the sky. "Does everyone have rain gear? We might get a little wet here." She studied the cloud formations.

June scoffed. "I checked the weather. We're good until late night. We'll push on while we have good light."

Black clouds piled overhead as they picked their way along the trail. Holly tugged on Cal's pack at one point. The group stretched out along the trail, forming smaller bunches as they hiked. As usual, Sam and Bert strolled a way ahead, while June and Asa lagged behind.

"If it rains, do we go back?" Tension filled her words. Hiking was not her activity of choice, and doing it in the rain sounded miserable.

Cal patted her on the back. "We've got rain gear, and if anything comes down, it'll be short-lived." He gently squeezed her. "We'll be fine."

"Hey, none of that," Sam jeered from behind them. "This is a G-rated hike."

Cal waved with one finger before hooking his arm in Holly's. "Once we get to the split in the trail, I want to show you the view. If we time it right, it looks spectacular at sunset."

His idea sounded great, but returning to the inn in the dark worried Holly. The hike consisted of a long walk uphill, no climbing involved, but walking an unfamiliar path without a light source did not sound appealing.

"If you say so," she curled into him a little, as best she could, considering their pace. "But I'm a little apprehensive here. Will the split trail add time to our hike?" She glanced at the sky. The darkening clouds and setting sun left her with a sense of dread.

"I promise it will be fine." Cal increased the pace, as if trying to catch up with Kinley. Holly followed suit, matching his speed. The faster they reached the top, the sooner they could go home.

Cal waved to June as he led Holly down the split trail. He never checked to see if June saw him. Not that it mattered. Trail C was a cake walk, and the group had traveled the path many times.

If they felt up for it, they chose the slightly more treacherous split, which led to the best view on the mountain, in his opinion. The ridge at the end of the trail opened up, and Bakersville lay displayed below in its entirety. The town appeared tiny and quaint, right off a Christmas card or a hokey romance novel. Holly could snap a few pictures for her article if she planned to talk about the town as she'd mentioned. He loved that view more than any other in the world.

Bakersville was home.

But also, Cal wanted to share his hometown with this lovely lady. Yes, she was a city girl, but if she fell in love with Bakersville, so much the better.

"Are we there yet, Cal?" she asked, as they crossed a plain planked bridge over a rushing stream. "Where are we going?"

"We're checking out a view of the town. The route is great, a few waterfalls, a few streams." He waved at the creek rushing by.

"The water looks a little high." Holly ran over the makeshift bridge as if it were collapsing behind her. "Is it safe?"

Cal sighed, disappointed that his reassurance fell on deaf ears. "It's spring runoff. Everything is running a little high. There's no threat of flash floods. I checked before we left."

He grasped her hands and pulled her close, loving the new intimacy between them. "Let's enjoy a private walk through a beautiful forest, listen to the birds, observe the spring flowers, and indulge in quiet alone time."

Holly twisted in his grip. Not moving away but appearing coy. "I assumed you didn't enjoy the quiet. You are always go, go, go." She closed the distance between them. "A real man in motion."

He took the advantage and placed another soft kiss on her lips. He wanted it to be a slow-cooker event. He always rushed in too fast with new women, and most of the time scared them off. Holly understood his energy level, though she didn't share it.

She responded to his lips by snuggling in, pressing against him, but neither deepened the kiss. They were exploring, finding their way.

He loved it.

He grasped her hand and headed further into the woods. The tree line closed in around them. New leaves shone everywhere, dappling the sunlight along the path. Talk about romantic. He hoped she was eating it up because he sure was.

"You hike a lot?" she asked, her voice a little distracted.

He glanced at her as she swiveled her head everywhere, taking in the scenery. *Excellent, his plan appeared to be working.*

"About once a week, barring bad weather. If it's super rainy or snowy, we beg off. I don't love a super cold trek, but Bert does. He has tons of wild winter gear. I swear he spends all his profits from the garage trying to find the perfect snowsuit for deep weather hikes." Cal chuckled.

"Everyone needs a hobby," Holly quipped and squeezed his hand.

After about half an hour, they came to another wooden bridge. Holly's heartbeat steadied. The structure appeared sturdier than the first bridge. The logs were tied together along the bottom with woven rope handrails to either side. It spanned a fast-moving creek. The water roared inches underneath the floor.

"Okay, this one looks safe," Holly mused, "but the water doesn't."

Cal peered over the side. "It's a good half a foot down. And this thing"—he bounced up and down a few times—"is in great shape."

Holly gripped the rope rail as if her life depended on it. "Jesus! Never do that again. Promise me you will never do that again." She didn't love heights, and rushing rivers weren't much better.

In the end, the rough walking and the time felt worth it. As they cleared the tree line, the world opened up below, in a sparkling New York state detail. The roads resembled tiny rivers, the trees, and the green covered the landscape with sparkling blue blobs of ponds and lakes here and there. Nestled in the center sat Bakersville, a shining picture-perfect town surrounded by a vast green landscape.

It stole Holly's breath away.

Chapter Eleven

"So beautiful!" Holly breathed in the cool air and marveled at the view. She could get used to such a view.

"We already did the campfire thing, but…"

She turned to Cal.

He held a bottle, two glasses, and a bag of jelly beans.

Heat crawled up her neck into her cheeks. *Who is this guy?* Mister Romance and Cuteness. Of course, she'd enjoy the view with him and live in the moment. She did not know where this thing might end up. She didn't believe the budding thing between them would go anywhere, but resisting him appeared to be almost impossible.

Cal produced a plaid blanket and a tarp. He put the tarp down first, followed by the blanket. He arranged a bowl and the glasses. He removed the cork with a quiet pop and poured the golden liquid into the glasses. The scene looked perfect, and Holly paused to drink it in.

Cal seemed to be a sweet man, too sweet. He was perfect, kind, caring, friendly, fun, and energetic. Holly shook her head. How could he be so amazing and still single? *So, what's wrong with him?*

She frowned, her gaze moving off into space.

Cal watched the joy leech from Holly's expression. He'd pushed too far. He always did. When he liked a woman, he completely threw himself at her. Usually, she'd say no or put up a stop sign.

But Holly followed along with him. They had such chemistry. Each time they hung out, he felt it. Her laugh, her intelligence, her patience. And he'd blown it with too big a romantic gesture too soon.

It might've been a mistake to leave the group and detour, but the idea of presenting the view to her alone called to him. They only had a short time together. She'd leave tomorrow night. Too much too soon, his usual game. Maybe the champagne influenced, or perhaps the jelly beans. He sighed, resigned he'd messed it up before they'd begun.

He'd try to save the moment. He raised a glass to the sunset. The light seemed to fade faster than it should have. "Here's to a great article and some new business."

She raised her own glass, her eyes refocusing. "Oh. Yes." She bit her lip. "To new business and prosperity." Her neck and cheeks still appeared a little pink. Was the blush from his lame toast, or did she hope for more?

No. Stop going down that road. Finish the hike, head home, finish the interview tomorrow with his grandma, and then say goodbye.

They clinked glasses, the atmosphere heavy with sorrow. Cal sipped his champagne, not enjoying it. They'd had more intimacy in the kitchen, making the beans.

Oh, the beans!

He pulled the small bag from his pack and dumped the contents in the bowl. He kept his attitude cheery and fun. “I have pre-selected a variety of flavors to go with our drinks while we ponder the view.” He grinned, brandishing a vibrant red bean. He passed it to her. In his head, he’d hand-fed her the beans, but no way would he try it now.

The bean, an oversized one, looked ridiculously huge in her hand. She feigned a smile and bit it in half. The juice in the middle squirted out all over her hands. Holly let out a gasp and tipped her head back to keep the trickles from running down her face.

Cal scrambled for a napkin from his pack and crawled over to help. He dabbed at her face, apologizing for not warning her.

Suddenly, they were deliciously close. He was on his hands and knees in front of her, and she sat with her legs folded to the side. Holly’s gaze met his. Heat rolled over his body.

Maybe all was not lost.

“Here,” he said, his voice gruff. He picked up her glass and handed it to her. “Chew slowly but take a sip.”

She did as he bade. The moment felt so intimate, the urge to ravage her right there almost overwhelmed him. He wanted to cover her with kisses and forget about jelly beans and mountain views for a few hours.

Holly's eyes closed, and her face took on an expression of pure pleasure. He wanted to see her make that face everywhere—over dinner, on a hike, in bed.

She chewed the bean with care, meeting his gaze as she swallowed. "My God, Cal. Champagne and strawberry-filled jelly beans? It's a million-dollar idea."

Cal frowned, sad she focused on money, not him or the pleasure of eating a perfect treat. He lowered his head and backed away from her, ashamed of his lust. She came here to do a job, not hop in the sack with the subject of her article.

He didn't get more than an inch before she had two handfuls of his shirt. He blinked hard as she pulled him toward her. She pressed her mouth against his, strawberry and champagne on her lips.

Perfect.

Then the skies opened up.

"Holy shit." Holly pushed away from Cal as cold water dumped over her like a bucket. She scrambled to her feet, unsure what to do.

Cal moved quickly, grabbing the blanket.

The sudden rain blinded Holly until a sheet of blue flew over her head. The torrent of water ceased. Cal stood beside her, huddled together with the tarp over their heads.

"Here!" Cal had to shout over the sound of the downpour. "Get low. It'll keep us a little dryer, if we hunker down."

Instinctively, she followed his lead. She had no idea what was happening. Hiking was one thing, but in this downpour? Holly hated storms. It terrified her to her bones. She'd always hide in a quiet room or under the covers if a thunderstorm struck.

Now they were outside in one, with no shelter, no help. They would be washed away. They'd end up falling over the side of the mountain. They'd be struck by lightning. Terror climbed up her legs to her chest. Her eyes stung with tears, and she gave in.

She clung to Cal with a ferocity she didn't know was in her. She probably put him in a headlock in her panic, but she didn't care. They had situated themselves precariously on the top of a mountain in a downpour without an umbrella or shelter anywhere. They might die up here. Why had she agreed to go on the trip?

Cal's lips pressed against her ear. "You're okay. We're okay. It's just rain. No lightning. We can sit here all night if need be."

"All night?" Her voice squeaked to a high C. "Wha?" Her indignation faded as she met his cool blue gaze.

His expression appeared serene, the epitome of calm. The hyper-frantic guy who did everything at a thousand miles an hour, gazed at her with a small smile and no fear. He looked as if he was trying not to laugh at a hilarious situation.

"Guess I didn't check the weather well enough before we left. June is usually on top of the precipitation situation. Apparently, not today."

Holly only heard about every other word through the deluge, but she parsed out his meaning. His calm helped, his arms around her even more so.

Slowly, her heart stopped racing, though her tension in her limbs remained. The temperature dropped ten degrees despite their tight quarters. Her body shook as she curled herself small and tight against Cal. He hugged her tighter, whispering sweet, calming words.

Her mind whirled with a thousand questions. Did Cal feel this way all the time? She studied him, at his serene, amused face, and calmed further. He leaned over and kissed her lightly as the rain redoubled its efforts.

She squealed and curled into his chest as tightly as possible. The air filled with a ridiculous level of booms and crashes, even without thunder and lightning.

And the darkness felt worse. It felt as if someone turned the lights off, and they were plunged into pure black. Huddled in the dark, all she could do was hold on.

The sounds around them escalated by the second. A wild rushing overpowered the rain and the wind, like a train headed right for them.

This is it. We are about to be swept off the cliff and fall to our deaths.

She glanced at Cal, ready to tell him how much she liked him, loved his hyper behavior, and his brilliant brain. Not to mention his sexy lumberjack look and red hair. She sucked in a breath.

Outside their makeshift shelter, a terrible wrenching sound filled the air as if a dozen trees crashed to the ground at once. Holly screamed, and Cal muttered "Jesus" under his breath, his voice hinting at a Scottish accent.

Holly buried her head in his shoulder and sobbed. The rain, the crashing, the noises… She felt terrified beyond anything she'd experienced before. Her brain froze. She held on to Cal in a death grip, unable to let go, unable to wrap her mind around the situation. She cried into his shirt with wild abandon.

Cal held Holly as tightly as she gripped him. The poor woman shook like a leaf. He hated himself for hauling her up here. No one could predict a flash shower.

But man, someone in the group should've kept a better eye on the weather.

He worried for a second about the rest of the group. Were they able to keep safe during the onslaught? There was no other word for it. The rain pelted down relentlessly, heavy and cold.

The crash beyond their shelter threw him. He stopped himself from jumping up and running off with Holly in tow. The noise sounded as if the trees were snapping off and hitting the ground or the stream. He wanted to throw off the tarp and examine the damage. It took every ounce of his strength to stay here with Holly and ride it out.

Her sobs slowed with the pace of the rain. In about ten minutes, both quieted completely.

He glanced at her, hardly able to see with the dim light filtering through the tarp. The sun had set, and he needed flashlights.

"How ya doing, reporter?" He flashed her a warm grin. "Look at all the new ideas for your story!" His response laugh sounded a little maniacal.

Holly shoved him, knocking him over. The tarp went with him, and she gasped as the sky opened above them.

He paused for a second, glancing up. Not a single cloud appeared in the sky. Stars winked above, and a half-moon showed in the lower section. "Huh."

Holly stood, blinking, gazing around at the softly lit landscape. "It's as if we went through some kinda time vortex." Her voice, sounding awed and steady, reassured Cal. She no longer seemed terrified out of her wits, and the stone on his heart lifted.

He sat up, taking stock of their surroundings. The edge of the cliff loomed far off to their right. They were far enough away to be safe if anything had crumbled. Still, he'd keep both of them far from the edge. The rangers would check the stability, a task beyond his pay grade.

Branches and leaves blanketed the ground as if time leaped forward during the storm and dropped them back in autumn. He narrowed his gaze, searching for a scrap of the picnic blanket and basket. No luck. It probably sailed halfway down the mountain.

They were safe, in one piece, no injuries. He couldn't ask for more. He stood, stretching after such a long time in a crouch. Holly stood nearby, her arms folded over her chest.

Their clothes didn't have a dry spot on them, and the rapid decrease in temperature only added to the rotten situation. Holly's teeth chattered like a typewriter. He scanned the branches and debris, too wet for a fire. In truth, they needed to hike down the mountain to a warm car.

He grabbed his pack and scouted again for hers. His backpack was soaked through, but thank goodness for waterproof lights. "Did your pack make it under the tarp?" he asked, scanning the ground, ignoring the whipping wind and roaring river. She shook her head. "Oh, well."

With the rain and the spring runoff, the water in the river probably hit a foot over max. It flooded most years, but usually only at the top of the mountain. By the time the rushing water hit the bottom, the tributaries stole the flow and dissipated any danger.

"Cal…" Holly stared into the darkness toward the trail.

"If we can find the pack, we can use my flashlights for the trip to the car." He pulled his out and clicked the button a few times. "They're supposed to be waterproof, but that was a hell of a rainstorm."

"Cal…"

He searched through his oversized Hyperlight pack. Holly had rolled her eyes at the size of it, and June scolded him for carrying too much. His busy brain refused to leave anything behind. What if he needed a small frying pan? It could be a great weapon, but also fantastic for frying fish. Then he might need…

"Cal!" Holly's bark of his name brought him around.

He glanced at her. Her arms hung at her side, all angst gone from her expression. Instead, her eyebrows knit, and worry lines surrounded her frown, making her appear furious and scared at the same time.

"The bridge is gone."

Chapter Twelve

Holly flung her arm toward the remains of the wooden bridge over the gorge. The structure lay in the water. No, not just in the water. It hung on by a single rope from the opposite side of the river. Most of it was missing, a few logs, a few scraps of rope tossed and turned in the churning water. The river, which lapped all the way up to the bank's edge, crashed downstream like white water rapids.

She dropped her arm to her side. They were trapped—freezing cold, wet, lost, and alone on a mountain. She spun to Cal, hoping beyond hope he'd laugh and point out another path down. Something that didn't require the hike they'd done on the way up. A paved path with handrails, towels, and snack machines.

"Cal…" she said again, when he stared slack-jawed at the ruin of the bridge.

"That thing… They built with… Damn." His last word quieted into a whisper. "I'm not…" His gaze met hers, and she knew all was lost. They'd have to wait for rescue and hope the storm ended, the flooding receded, and the bears remained sleeping.

A sensation like she might leave her body floated over her skin. *This isn't happening*. She was not stuck in the woods, in the dark.

Trapped.

They were trapped.

Her gaze danced all over the place, but the growing darkness revealed nothing. A whimper escaped her lips.

His hand fell gently on her shoulder, eased onto it as if not trying to spook a nervous horse. She was beyond nervous, more like panicked and frantic.

"We're okay, Holly. Other people know we are out here, and we have cell phones. Neither of us is hurt or sick."

She whined again as her gaze frantically jumped from one shadow to another. Do wolves live in the Adirondacks? What about mountain lions? They were on a mountain. Her body shook violently, and Cal wrapped her in his arms.

"Are you hurt?" he whispered in her ear. "Tell me. I can help. If you're scared, I've got you. We have the tarp, a little food, and water." He held her in a tight hug, rubbing circles over her back. It took way too long for her body to settle.

Not an outdoor person, but she'd occasionally go for a simple hike or a beginner-level rock climb. Then straight to the coffee bar afterward. She exercised in the place God intended—the gym.

Now she was stranded on a mountain in the middle of…

"I'll call June to see if they are okay. Then the ranger station." Cal placed a delicate kiss on her cheek, and her shoulders dropped a few inches. "Check your phone, too."

Robotically, as if none of her joints worked properly anymore, Holly pulled her cell from her back pocket. She handed it to Cal with the water dripping down the side.

"It might work," he said, flashing a grin at her.

She gave him a dead stare.

He tried a couple of times to get her phone to turn on with no avail. "Bring any rice?" He quipped, but she snatched the device from his hand and shoved it in her pocket. She stepped away, her arms wrapping around her body.

"Now what?"

He held up his phone. "Also, dead." She grimaced, her head bowing. Cal pulled her in again. "Bad choice of words. I'm sorry. We'll see how bad the river is. There's a chance we can cross downstream." He glanced around. "We might find your pack."

Holly shrugged. Thoughts of starving in the woods without lights or warmth flashed in her head, and her legs turned to spaghetti. She sat down hard without the strength to complain.

Cal shrugged. "Okay then. We'll see what we have and what we need to do."

Holly shook her head. "Let me process…" She waved a hand as her words drifted off.

He crouched down in front of her, and lifted her chin in his hands. "You said you wanted to be a correspondent working in war zones and whatnot. Well, this is your on-the-job training."

Holly stared at him.

He was right. How could she go to the Middle East or Eastern Europe if a rainstorm threw her off? His blue eyes gazed at her without judgment. Cal didn't appear to be a guy to become upset with your faults or emotions. He seemed to be supportive and kind. He helped everyone. Currently, he was attempting to help her.

With two dead phones, calling the ranger station wasn't an option. Cal had planned for many scenarios, but not a torrential downpour. Or at least, not a surprise one. His pack contained plenty of rain gear—ponchos, another tarp, a mini tent, though no extra phones. Mentally, he added it to his list.

They were fine. No one was hurt.

The situation was fine. They'd survive it.

It was fine.

No need to panic.

He kept telling himself that until he believed it. They were not in a remote area. They were not on a regular path, but not stranded on all sides by steep cliffs. With the flashlights, he'd scout a way around the gorge. But it'd be safer to wait until daylight.

Holly might not be thrilled to discover they were stuck for the night. Better to stay in one spot than try to navigate alternate routes in the dark.

He pulled out a soggy headlamp and snapped it on. He aimed the light above Holly's head so as not to blind her. He finally saw her and pressed his lips to keep from laughing.

She looked like a drowned rat. Her beautiful hair hung in lank strips around her face, which appeared puffy from crying. Her clothes stuck to her, dripping. And her expression…

Good thing looks can't kill.

"So, uh, yeah, that was a thing. Are you feeling better?" He kept his words light, but she saw through him. His speech about being a war reporter bucked up her courage.

"Give it to me straight, Cal. How bad?"

He glanced around slowly, allowing the light to fall on everything. “It’s not bad. We’re in no danger here. Especially if we keep away from the edges.” He pointed the light where the bridge used to be and turned around to highlight the cliff edge. “So, here in the middle, no falling thousands of feet, nor getting flooded out.”

She crossed her arms. Her lips appeared a little blue in the flashlight glare. “How long?”

He nodded, loving that she was all business. He’d need her to keep them on the straight and narrow. His busy brain might try to construct a few random and dangerous plans. They should set their actions in stone before he thought too much about it.

“Tonight, at least. They won’t find us without GPS. June and company might have a dry phone or two. If they realize we’re missing, they’ll call the ranger station. But”—he waved at the former bridge—“since our way out is gone, I assume the rest of it washed downriver. Possibly breaking other bridges or blocking paths. I bet there are more trees down or other damage.”

He tapped his chin, not meeting her gaze. He didn’t want to witness any more fear. They were safe but not warm and dry. A situation he needed to remedy soon. Holly's shivering seemed to rattle her to the bone.

"So, we're stuck here, overnight."

"Yep." His mind bent with potential solutions.

"Cal." Her sharp tone stopped his wandering brain. "What do we have for supplies?"

All business. Nice.

"We should look for your pack. The wind was pretty wicked, though." He did a slow circle again, letting the light hit the perimeter.

"Cal." Sharp again. Holly understood his buzzing brain. "What do we have right now?"

He lifted his back. "A wet tarp, two sets of wet clothes, two wet phones."

She grimaced, appearing ready to throw her hands up. She turned away as if scanning for her backpack.

"In my pack, I have dry food, a canister of water, dry matches, two rain ponchos, and a little tent."

Holly spun to face him. "A tent? Why didn't you list that among our assets in the first place?"

Cal grinned at the movie reference. "Well, it's no wheelbarrow, but we'll both fit in it. It's an emergency shelter."

Holly flapped her hands. “And this isn’t an emergency?” She sighed heartily, but her eyes remained dry.

He’d rather have her angry than frightened. He didn’t like a helpless Holly. From what he’s seen of her, she was too put-together to be crying on the ground.

“So,” she continued. “We have shelter.” She pointed a finger at him. “Water. How about dry or warm clothes? Oh, and food.”

Cal squatted and pulled out the second tarp. The small rectangle fit just under the tent, not much use for them now. On it, he put a second flashlight, a variety of snacks, a flannel shirt, and a pair of wool camping pants.

He left the single thermos on the side of the pack. They could refill in the stream, but the bank might be unstable and crumble under their weight. If they found the wine glasses, then leaving them in the rain might work, too. If it rained again… He glanced at the sky. “We’ll put up the tent first.” He tapped the small roll.

“It can’t be a tent. There’s nothing to it.”

He shone the light over by the edge of the trees. “Emergency tent, remember? It’s tightly packed nylon. There aren’t any stakes, which means we have to put it between two trees." He scanned until he spotted a suitable location a few feet inside the tree line.

"Will they find us if we are in the woods? All these trees and rocks, and what if they fall over?" Panic climbed into Holly's voice again. She must not be much of a camper.

"We'll keep our lights on as much as we can. If we find your pack, we'll have two more lights." He stood and paced a few steps, ready to scout for the missing gear.

With a light touch, Holly grasped his arm. "Tent first."

He bowed. "As you wish."

Holly gazed at the small piece of nylon folded into an oblong pyramid. "That is not a tent. It's an umbrella someone mutated."

Cal sat back on his heels, glancing over the configuration. He scratched his head. Had he put it up before? Probably not, since it appeared to be well packed in the little bag. He'd never fit into it, much less the two of them together.

She shivered. Putting on warm clothes first might have been a better call, but then they'd have to strip. She didn't want to strip out here in the dark and the cold.

"It'll keep us covered for the night." Cal twanged the support string, tied to a nearby pine. "If it doesn't rain anymore, and the wind keeps down, we'll be cozy and warm." He grinned.

Yeah, body heat would be the ticket for the next eight hours. She almost welcomed being stuck in the woods if she could cuddle with Cal. Of course, she'd much rather do the cuddling in her hotel room.

While he fussed with the last details of the tent, putting rocks on the corners to hold it down, Holly grasped the second flashlight and slowly walked around. She'd found their life-saving tarp from the initial downpour, but no glasses, no champagne, no jelly beans, or bowl. More importantly, no backpack.

"Don't wander too far," Cal called after her, care in his tone.

He really was sweet. If she focused on him, she might get through this without losing it. Her emotions danced on the edge, but working the problem calmed her in the end.

"I don't see my pack anywhere. Is it worth it to search?"

She turned to watch him stand and stretch, a lovely sight, his long body stretching to his full height, his muscles working. The wet clothes, though probably freezing, highlighted the details.

She liked what she saw. Who'd have thought a man who created candy for a living would be in good shape?

"We can give a cursory search." He shrugged. "But the water was moving fast. I bet it's long gone. I couldn't see anything when the rain came down."

Holly tapped her lips, trying to remember. "I'm pretty sure I put it by the picnic blanket."

Cal moved to her side. "But I probably flung it when I grabbed the tarp."

She turned, and he stood right there. Up close, body heat radiated off him. She wanted to curl into his warmth.

"That was smart. You saved us a few headaches by doing it."

He shrugged. "But not the phones. Woulda been nice to save at least one phone. Anyway, we can scout for the pack a bit, but do it in tandem with searching for another path. There's a rougher one down from here. Not good for a night hike."

He grasped her hand and squeezed her fingers. "For safety" was what he said, but his voice sounded gruff and sexy.

Holly pressed her lips. They'd be stuck in the tiny tent soon enough. She glanced over at it. Why not go now?

"We don't have to look. I mean… If you think it's best to wait for daylight or rescue, why stress ourselves?" She twisted her fingers with his, trying to be coy but feeling like the most unsubtle person in the universe. "The pack is probably waterlogged, anyway. We could use the second water bottle, but we'll be fine with one." She smiled at him through her lashes, and he grinned.

"Maybe," he said, sliding closer. "We should change out of these wet things and settle in for the night."

The sound of rustling in the undergrowth stopped Holly cold. Her visions of bears and wolves hit her again. She wrapped her arms tight around Cal, pinning his arms to his side. "What was that?" Her words sounded like a ragged whisper, no longer playful or sexy. *Way to break the mood, Holly*, she chided herself.

"Probably a rabbit."

She couldn't help herself. "Not a bear?"

Cal shrugged. "Maybe a rescue."

Oh, and wouldn't that figure? They were so close to sexy time, and the ranger shows. Great, just her luck.

Then again, they could always warm up in her newly found tub at the B&B. That thought brought a smile to her lips.

Cal swept the light around. "The critters won't bother us. They probably didn't like the rain, either. I doubt the rangers would be here already." They paused for a second, wrapped together in cool night air.

A shiver spilled over Holly again. The frigid air pricked at her skin. She automatically grabbed her phone to check the temp.

"Signal?" he asked, peeling away from her.

"No, I tried to see the weather. I forgot…" She waved the dead phone. "I should've replaced it when the screen cracked."

He laughed. "Same. They're so expensive. Mine has a hole in the screen. I keep forgetting to replace it."

Holly slapped him playfully. “How can you forget your phone?”

He laughed, tugging her toward the little tent. “Have you met me? Forget is my middle name. Well, more like distracted, or ….”

“Or talkative.” Holly gave him her senior editor stare and walked beside him to the tent. “So, is it worth it to put on those dry clothes?” Wow, good job, Captain Obvious. She might as well ask him to strip right there.

“Yeah,” Cal answered with a low, casual tone. “Let’s take the wet stuff off before we go inside. I figure you put on the shirt, and I’ll do the pants. I have a couple of emergency blankets.”

Holly held up a hand, wishing he’d said, “I have several down comforters” instead of holding up a bright blue flannel shirt. The color caused her stomach to roll. Of all places to deal with her color-hating issues. *Oh well.* It would be warm.

Instead, she focused on the blankets. “You mean those silver sheets of nothing? Ugh.” She groaned and slumped. Then it dawned on her. Body heat would be the best source of warmth for the night.

A slow grin crawled across her lips.

"Oh, they work pretty well. Not super comfortable, but they keep the heat on ya." He removed two baggies from his pack and dug through the rest of the items. "I shoulda brought a flare. Never thought I'd need it…"

Holly plucked one of the baggies from his hand and tapped his chest with it. "I'm gonna trust you, because I'm freezing."

He nodded.

She drank him in. It might happen. It might not. But curled together half-naked in an emergency tent resembled a trashy romance plot. It might be fun to actually live out a scene from her favorite genre.

Oh, what the hell. Carpe diem and YOLO and the like.

Holly ripped open the plastic with her teeth, careful not to damage the blanket. She unfurled the little thing only to discover it ran to about six feet long. "Huh, bigger than expected." She caught his eye for half a second. "Hold it up."

Cal blinked, his brows furrowed. "What do…"

She flapped the blanket at him. "Hold each corner for me. No peeking."

Robotically, he grasped each edge and lifted the sheet, blocking her view of him.

“Perfect.” With lightning speed, she shucked off her wet shoes, pants, and shirt. She gulped a deep breath. The blue monstrosity would have to do. “Toss me the shirt.”

“Uh,” Cal said from behind the sheet. “I have to put the sheet down to get it.”

Holly laughed, actually laughed. Now that the terror had passed, her brain refused to find any logic or reason, and she giggled, practically giddy. Especially if she considered the two of them in the tent, cuddled up tight.

She snatched the sheet from his hand and wrapped it around herself. Not the most comfortable look, but it covered the important parts.

Cal stared, mouth open, eyes bugging out.

She allowed him a full five seconds to gawk, then shooed him. “Get the shirt.”

Without taking his gaze off her, he bent to his pack and pulled out the flannel shirt. The garment appeared to be more of a jacket with its fleece lining than a shirt. Holly was not splitting hairs as it looked warmer than she’d expected.

"Oh, gimmie." Her teeth started chattering again, and her body craved warmth beyond a reasonable measure for the situation, as if she'd die soon without some relief.

Cal handed it over and turned his back. *What a gentleman.*

She put the shirt on, leaving the blanket under it like a skirt. "Okay, now you."

He didn't turn, merely stripped off everything except a pair of tighty-whities. He donned the pants in a split second. He turned, bare-chested, and grinned at her.

Holly pulled in a breath, admiring the man's torso. No six pack, but the slim, trim body of a physically active man. His skin shone a rosy shade of pink in the light from her flashlight, perhaps from the cold, or the embarrassment of being half-naked in the woods.

They stood there in the dark and the cold for a minute. Holly didn't know what to do—yell, "Take me, you fool," or crawl into the tent? She bit her lip, considering.

Cal ran a hand through his hair, then shook it out. Water flew everywhere. "We should try to hang the clothes. So, they'll dry." He grabbed both piles and strung the items on the branches of the trees.

"Guess I'll go in?" She blinked at him and shrugged.

Why so awkward?

The chemistry between them should boil over. Instead, they were like two teens, unsure how the whole thing worked.

"Take the pack with you?" he asked, trying to wring out his jeans. "Use it as a pillow or something."

"Sure." Disappointment colored her words. No beautiful scene from a romance novel with two people forced together in an emergency. *Oh well.*

She grabbed the pack and crawled into the tent. The sides almost skimmed her body. No way would they both fit in here. She wiggled onto her stomach, putting the pack under her head.

Not a good pillow.

She turned on her side, hopefully leaving enough room for Cal to squeeze in.

Cal hung the last of the wet clothes on the branches. What the hell was he doing? A beautiful, intelligent woman sat inside the tent, almost naked, and he lingered outside.

What was the matter with him?

Holly was out of his league. His GED couldn't compare to her master's degree in journalism. The last woman he dated scoffed at his business and his lack of a college degree. How would he ever be enough for someone like Holly?

He didn't love a one-night stand. He wanted to be with her, but for more than a one-off. He liked her, but he was tired of temporary relationships that went nowhere.

He glanced at the tent, taking a moment to admire her feet sticking out of the flap. He smiled as she tucked them inside. If he stayed out here much longer, he'd freeze to death.

With a hitch in his breath, he headed to the tent. He had to go in, no choice about it. It would get colder, and traveling down the mountain tonight was out of the question. He'd stay on his side as much as possible and leave the poor woman alone.

Crawling into the tent, he noticed Holly curled on her side, the emergency blanket around her legs. "Is the blanket over your torso too?" His head spun, imagining the silver wrapped around her curvy body.

She turned toward him and squinted.

He furrowed his eyebrows at her, then realized he still wore the headlamp. "Oh, geez, I'm sorry." He snapped it off and pulled it off his head. "I forgot."

The total darkness of the night hit him. No light filtered through the walls. Embarrassment rolled over him. Naked, well, practically, in a tent with a beautiful woman. He swallowed hard.

"No worries." Her voice sounded muted in the blackness. "Keep it off. Or put the flashlight on between us. A nightlight of sorts." She shuffled in the blackness, and something of hers brushed against his chest.

Panic reared up again, but he shoved it down. "I'm going to put the headlamp at the door, in case one of us needs to…"

She giggled, the beautiful sound filling the small space. "What? Needs to pee?" More of her pressed against more of him. He hoped the utter lack of light encouraged bold behavior.

He wanted it to happen, but he didn't want Holly to disappear tomorrow. Maybe if he played the big, brave rescuing male, she'd fall for him and stay forever.

"Yeah, well, roaming around in the dark with a full bladder can be awkward at best. It doesn't hurt to have a light and be able to see the cliff or the bears."

She shifted over, her hand pressed against his chest. "Bears? Seriously? You said no bears. Are we in danger?"

Ah, a chance to be a hero.

But who was he kidding? He'd run from a bear as quickly as she. He was no hero. He was a confectioner, not a ranger, not a fireman. He made jelly beans.

"Probably no bears, Holly. But be careful." He lay down next to her. Her palm remained on his chest. He placed his hand over it, loving the heat it generated.

Her breathing slowed. "All right. Will we be okay? It's cold, even with the blanket."

"Oh yeah," he pulled out the second blanket from his pocket, opened it, and spread it over both of them.

She curled closer—not super close, not bodies pressed together close, but enough to make his breath catch.

Her breath warmed on his skin. “But it’s your blanket. Won’t you be cold?”

He shook his head, struggling to form words. Of course, she failed to see him shake his head in the dark. “No. It’s better to put it over both of us. It reflects our own body heat back at us. Two bodies, more heat.”

The air in the tent changed immediately. Holly pushed away a little while remaining under the blanket with him.

“I’m making you uncomfortable,” she said flatly, sounding disappointed. “I didn’t mean to push anything. I…well…”

He shifted. The tent felt cramped, and his height didn’t help matters. “We need to share body heat, and talk…”

“Isn’t that what people say after…”

Her body moved against his, and his senses hit overload. He needed to get their situation under control. His impulsive brain said, “kiss her blue,” but his rational brain, what was left after being almost naked next to the smartest, sexiest woman he’d met in a long time, said, “slow it down.”

He should listen to the rational voice.

"Okay, Holly..." He cleared his throat. "I didn't plan anything. I, uh, I like you." *God, why was it so hard to throw it out there*? "I'm not good at planning, but I'm glad we got stuck. I wanted a chance to be alone, like when we made the candy. We never seem to talk about much but the candy shop or the people in town, and I'm always zooming around fixing things and..."

Her finger pressed against his lips, shushing him. "I didn't believe you worked out a deal with Mother Nature to strand us here. But I'm glad we got to be alone. I like you, too." She moved closer. The rustle of the silver sheet sounded loud in the small space.

He tightened his grip on her hand. He'd forgotten he held it. "Cool. I mean, I want to know you more than just in a tent in the woods. Know what I mean?"

There. He'd spilled his guts.

Hopefully, she'd understand he didn't care for one-night stands.

Chapter Thirteen

Holly slid her hand from his chest to his shoulder. "I understand, Cal. We've had some chemistry the past few days. Are you saying you wanna date?"

His shoulder moved up and down under her hand. A shrug. "I wanna be a gentleman. I'm feeling… and you are…" He put his hand around her waist and pulled her closer. "And it's very close in here. And you're leaving tomorrow."

She sighed, pressing her cheek against his bare chest. *There's the rub, huh?* If she became a correspondent, she'd be in one town one day and gone the next. A serious relationship didn't work with her career goals. Perhaps he'd be open to…

"I want to travel the world and report on the meaty issues. Wars, terrorists, conflict, riots, bombings. I can't do that in Bakersville." She stroked his cheek. "But we're here now and…"

He pressed his cheek against the top of her head. "I'm not proposing or anything. Plattsburg has an excellent paper, and so does Burlington. It's not too far. I'm not saying you should move. But I gotta stay here. Man, I just thought we could…"

He bent and kissed her. It was the sweetest thing she'd ever experienced. Most of the men she met through the magazine and in college were newsies. Wham, bam, thank you, ma'am, and gone in the morning.

But this guy…

He wanted to spend time with her. The man pressed against her, practically naked, and did *not* take advantage even when she signaled her openness to a romp in the woods.

He was a gentleman, a little hyper, and a bit of a rambler, who helped his friends all the time. He worked hard at his business and had no problem allowing his employees to help him run it. He'd taken a legacy from his family and run with it. He was sweet, successful, and interested in her beyond a three-day meeting.

Oh, my God. I'm falling for him. Stupid spring fever.

She pressed herself fully against him, letting the kiss linger for too long. "Cal. We'll see where it goes."

Apparently, all he needed boiled down to an openness for more.

His hands roamed over her sides and arms as he pressed into a deeper kiss. He slid under her shirt and tugged at the blanket around her.

She snorted as he attempted to remove it. "I never should have…" He didn't allow her to finish. A tearing sound filled the tent as the blanket pulled free.

"No worries," he breathed into her hair. "It's easily removed." He plunged down to kiss her again.

She shifted closer, loving the touch of his hands on her bare skin.

For a man who'd been hesitant to move to the next level, he certainly wasn't holding back now. He kissed her with a fervor that tingled her toes.

His hands explored her body, running over her legs and under her shirt. It seemed as if he didn't know where to touch her first, and he touched her everywhere instead. It seemed his hyper brain was good for this activity, too.

The size of the tent left little room to move, but he managed to turn her on her back.

"Holly…" he said breathlessly. "You are so beautiful."

She giggled again as his mouth moved down her neck and across her collarbone. "You can't see me in the dark."

"True," he said between soft wet kisses on each bare breast. "But when one sense is out of commission, the others compensate. For example, touch." He pulled one nipple into his mouth, sucking and rolling the tip. "Or sound…" He whispered in her ear, his breath hot and heavy. "I'm going to make you so happy, Holly. You'll be begging for more."

The heat of his breath on her ear, the touch of his hands on her breasts, sent a shock through her. Her body thrummed, and she wrapped one leg around his. "God, Cal. Don't stop."

"I have no intention of stopping." His fingers traced down her torso to her panties. "We should've taken those off," he whispered in her ear. "They appear to be wet, too."

He slipped a finger between the fabric and her folds. Electricity pulsed through her again. Heat bloomed over her skin, and to her surprise, she was close already. No one had ever brought her so fast.

She ripped at the rest of the blanket and the shirt, overheating in the tent.

He touched her with great care, using his mouth on her neck, her collarbone, her shoulders, and his fingers played with her folds. He built a slow rhythm that drove her wild.

Finally, she called his name, almost in a scream, and he plunged his fingers inside, pressing on her clit, forcing her orgasm. She bucked and writhed under his touch, seeing stars as she came hard on his fingers.

Oh my God. We kicked the tent over.

But after a minute, the stars faded, and only she and Cal remained in the dark, panting, breathing, content.

Cal would've given anything to see Holly crash over. The dark made it exciting and dangerous, but it also hid her expressions and her body from view. Next time, they'd go with tons of lights on, in broad daylight. He hummed with desire just thinking about it.

He slid his hand to her hip and rolled to his side. She curled against him, the scent of her sex filling the tent. He groaned. Man, he'd love to give her more, lick her senseless under the moonlight. But the cold would never allow it.

"Cal." Her voice sounded low, willowy, as if she were drunk. Intoxicated Holly would be fun to see. He lamented the loss of the champagne. Her hand stroked the front of his pants, and his brain snapped back to their immediate activities.

He wanted her, to bury himself inside her, and make her come again. He hesitated, unsure if …

Apparently, she had her own agenda. She untied his pants and reached for him. He ended up hanging his wet underwear, leaving him commando under the wool pants. She made happy sounds, finding him ready and easily accessible.

Her touch sent tendrils of heat through his body. He

bit his lip. It always went wrong here. He became too excited, too horny, and rushed the woman, pushed her too far, too soon. He had a hard time cooling his hyper brain.

"Holly, I…" He swallowed hard as her hand stroked him, tugging a little on the upward movement. He wouldn't last long if she kept it up. Her hands felt like heaven, and he wanted to go there.

"Cal, what do you need?" She buried her face in his neck, gently sucking on his skin while her hand continued to move over the length of him.

"Holly…" His voice faltered. "You are the most intelligent, beautiful woman I've ever met." He thrust into her hand, unable to hold back any longer. Not what he'd hoped for, but they had all night. His breath stuttered as he came in her hand, her name like a prayer on his lips.

They lay there together, side by side, in the cooling darkness. Her hand rested on his stomach, his arms wrapped around her.

He listened to her breath, blissful and content, but a little embarrassed that it ended quickly.

"I'm sorry," he muttered into her hair. "You are so…"

A small laugh escaped her lips. "No man has ever said such things in bed. Usually, it's a grunt or 'oh baby' or something. She kissed his neck again, and a deep passion stirred inside him. "You are a unique man, Callum McIntyre."

He bent and kissed her, all feelings of embarrassment evaporating.

Holly shifted a little. The tent was so small that lying face-to-face felt restrictive. She wished she could turn to spoon, but disturbing the moment would be a tragedy.

Not yet.

Not before.

She also didn't want to press him. Recovering after such a huge orgasm might take hours. He already seemed a little chagrined he'd come into her hand. Well, the tent absolutely did not have room for a blow job, which she was dying to do.

With a smile, she opted to tell him so.

"Cal, I wish we had a larger tent. I can't get at you in here." She curled in again, her hand reaching for him. She stroked him in long, languid strides, enjoying the soft skin as it enlarged in her hand.

"If we had the room," she purred, "I'd take you in my mouth and set your world on fire."

He was completely hard in an instant. "Holly," he breathed as if shocked but also excited. "We…"

She quickened her pace. She wanted him inside her, but condoms were necessary. If she sucked him off, there'd be no need for a condom.

"Do you have …" Her words trailed off, hoping he'd understand her meaning. His hand found her breast, kneading it slowly, delicately.

He cleared his throat, "Promise you won't be mad?"

Warning lights fired in her head. *Mad? About what?*

"I brought some. You know, in case, we… Like what if…" He kissed her forehead. "I don't want you to think I expected or…"

She pulled away, pressing a finger to his lips. "You know what your problem is, Cal?" she asked using her anchorwoman voice. "You talk too much."

He snorted. "In the backpack."

It took her two seconds to find the box and remove the wrapper from a condom. She rolled it on him to the sound of appreciative groans.

"Are you sure?" he asked, his voice pure gravel.

"God, yes," She spun him on top of her, wrapping her legs around his waist. He slid inside her in a single movement.

"Holly." He sounded strangled. "You sure? Because I didn't do…"

She thrust her hips up, pushing him deeper. "You did plenty." She cupped his chin in her hand. "Focus."

He grinned, bent to kiss her, and took her on the wildest ride she'd had in a long time. His contortions spun her into the stratosphere, and she came hard, then again. Cal didn't stop. He was like a machine.

God, the second time is always marvelously long. She could get used to this.

He whispered her name and pulled her legs up to his shoulders. Hovering over her, he buried himself deep inside her and collapsed on top of her.

He touched her face with a gentle caress, and Holly was done. He was the guy. Even with his quirks and his small-town life. She wanted him, now and forever.

And didn't that just mess with her big plans?

Chapter Fourteen

Cal woke hours later, his skin cold everywhere it didn't touch Holly. He lay on his back, Holly curled against his side, one arm and one leg thrown over him. Dim light filtered through the sides of the tent, which hung askew after the activity of last night. He glanced at her, a smile spreading over his face.

His whole body relaxed seeing the beautiful woman in his arms. If it ended here, he'd deal. Last night had been magical, and he'd do it all again in a heartbeat.

He let out a long sigh, pulling her a little tighter. A few more minutes of bliss before they were forced to hike down the mountain and return to their real lives.

Holly stirred next to him, her mouth finding his neck. It didn't take her long to discover what he enjoyed. Wet lips on his throat drove him into overdrive. He rolled her over onto her back, kissing her, touching her, his cock as hard as a rock.

They moved together as if they'd been partners forever. Their bodies singing praises of each other, their skin hot with contact, their brains mush.

Finally, Cal reached for a condom when a loud whistle rang in the air.

"Found them," a male voice called out.

Cal met Holly's eyes, which were as large as saucers. His own jaw hit the floor. They scrambled for the clothes. They could never get dressed in the small space. Holly straddled his chest, pulling on the shirt while he humped up his hips, trying to put the pants on over his erection. It didn't help that her naked body hovered over him. Their gazes met, and heat flashed again.

"To be continued," Holly murmured, rolling off him to scramble into her panties.

"You two decent in there?" It was Sam, who'd have no problem whisking the tent away for a laugh.

Cal grabbed the scraps of the silver blanket, thrust it at Holly, and repeated a mantra of baseball stats to calm his body. The wool pants, though warm, would highlight his condition.

"Knock, knock," Sam called from next to the tent. The man's shadow covered the structure.

With one last glance at Holly, Cal pushed back the flap and crawled out of the tent. He turned and held out a hand for Holly. She grasped it and allowed him to draw her outside. Automatically, he pulled her against his side, blocking her from the frigid air.

"Well." June stood by their drying clothes. "Looks like you had quite the night."

Holly said nothing, merely glared at June.

Cal agreed. They were too old to be teased about sex. Nevertheless, heat rose in his cheeks.

"How's everyone else? Did anyone get hurt? Were you stuck, too?"

June held up a hand. Her travel cast appeared a little worn but still intact. "Asa got caught in a bit of a landside. Some scrapes and bruises. But it's not too bad. No emergency until we noticed you two disappeared."

Her voice held a "you're in trouble with the teacher" note.

Cal shrugged. "Sorry. We didn't detour far." He waved over where the bridge used to be. "I didn't think for a second you'd miss us, much less have to rescue us."

Sam snorted, examining the tent. "You two didn't need rescuing. Just a bigger tent." He laughed hard. He must have seen the condom box. "Or maybe you didn't."

Cal let the jokes roll off his back. He didn't care, but he glanced at Holly to ensure she didn't feel humiliated. She hovered near the entrance to the tent.

"Can I get some pants, please?" she asked, raising a hand. "Mine were soaked and unwearable. Thank you very much." Her tone sounded so commanding that no one dared challenge her.

June thumped her enormous pack on the ground. She was in true rescue mode, sore ankle or no. She dug inside and pulled out a couple of pairs of thermal leggings and pants. She tossed one to Holly and found a flannel shirt for Cal.

He grabbed it happily, a little self-conscious to be half-naked on the mountain, but nothing else bothered him. He didn't care if his friends knew he and Holly had hooked up. He didn't care about being trapped in the woods. He was grateful to find his friends here with clothes and…

The smell hit him like a steamroller, but Holly stepped in front of him.

"Coffee." She moaned the word the same way she'd said his name last night.

He grinned, loving how he ranked right up there with a hot beverage.

Once dressed, jacketed, and blanketed with hot cuppas in their paws, the group settled into a chat about the storm and the damage. June related how Asa slipped and landed in the local hospital, but everyone else in the group survived just fine, merely got soaked. She shared a few more details when a loud whistle echoed over the ridge.

Five more people emerged from the woods, packs and walking sticks in hand, a ranger leading the way. Greetings rang all around when a third group of would-be rescuers arrived.

Cal grinned, recognizing faces from the fire brigade, the pizza shop, the diner, and even Suzanne and Wendy.

Those two rushed him and crushed him in a tight embrace.

"Jesus, I thought we lost you. We heard reports of the creek rising and…" Suzanne tightened her grip until Cal gasped in pain.

As per usual, she pushed away from him as if she'd never shown him a bit of affection. She turned on June and laid into her. "How dare you put people on that trail in that weather? You're supposed to be the expert, and here they are trapped overnight and…"

Cal wrapped an arm around her, quelling her tirade. June scowled at Suzanne. The two held no love between them.

"We're fine."

Suzanne protested, but Cal cut her off. "And I planned from the start to sneak over here to have a little champagne in the moonlight. June is completely innocent."

Suzanne swatted at him. "What were you thinking?" She glared at him, her eyes narrowing to slits. She glanced at him up and down and spun to scrutinize Holly. She opened her mouth to speak, but he placed a careful hand over it.

Suzanne saw everything. Not that he tried to hide anything from her, but he didn't want her to berate him in public about his nightly activities.

The entire time, Holly sat on the ground with her cup of coffee, her eyes darting back and forth between the combatants. He could see her reporter brain working.

When Holly unfolded herself from the ground, her brain stuttered, trying to process all that had happened. The entire town showed up with food, clothing, and blankets. Her gaze darted from face to face, as her mind clicked.

"So, there's another path to get here?" she asked, her gaze alighting on each person.

June huffed. "Not an easy one, but there's a secondary trail."

Holly tapped her chin. "But the three groups appeared from three directions. So…

The ranger grinned. "I guessed you might be here. I sent those without busted ankles through the woods in a few directions in case you were elsewhere."

June's face turned maroon. "It's not busted. It's sprained, and it happened two weeks ago when I…"

The ranger raised a hand to cut her off. He turned to Holly. "So yes, we all came from various directions."

She raised her eyebrows. Three largish groups of townspeople converged on their location. She assumed they volunteered. "All of you came out to help us?" She'd bet that not one of those lovely people was here because she, a reporter, got stuck on the mountain.

"Of course, we did!" Sam threw his hands up. "It's Cal." His face reddened realizing his slip. "And you, too."

She glanced at the group again. They cheered and talked, picking up the debris from the camp, Cal helping right alongside everyone. His cheerful voice thanked people. He gave hugs all around. Not one of those lame one-armed guy hugs. He squeezed people, and they hugged him back.

The epiphany hit her: They loved him.

Not a "prodigal son" kind of thing, but as if he were the heart of the town. He did for them in little ways. She assumed his repairs, advice, and saving moves were the usual. And the people knew it. He saved them frequently. No wonder they dropped everything to rescue him.

Holly pressed her lips, trying to stop the threatening tears. Bakersville was a real community, almost out of a storybook. A town that took care of its own, gave back, and loved.

But they weren't perfect.

Look at how June and Suzanne faced off. But they pulled together for Cal. Did they do that for others? If they understood how much Russ struggled with his bed-and-breakfast, would they save him, too?

What would they do with a reporter who had no idea what to do with her life after visiting their weird little town and falling in love with their favorite confectioner?

Every fiber of her being said stay in Bakersville. Screw big scary news stories and write about the summer tourists, celebrities visiting Lake Placid, and town events. Or cover big stories like "Candy Shop Guy Stuck on the Mountain."

She closed her eyes, and tears spilled down her cheeks. The town was terrific, and her heart said, *"Stay with him, the town, help Russ, eat at the diner, shop at the general store, learn to make more candy."*

She hurriedly brushed at her lashes, turning to gaze out over the ridge to the beautiful sunlit view of the Adirondacks.

Yes, the place appeared to be special. She needed to make sure it was real.

A light touch on her arm, and Cal's warm breath in her ear, stopped her whirling brain. "You okay?" he asked, his tone gentle, sweet.

"They came for you. All these people." More traitorous tears dropped. "How does that happen? I've covered dog shows where people got into fist fights and plywood derbies sabotaged by bitter parents. I've seen nothing like this."

Cal ducked his head and planted a kiss on her forehead. "Well, we don't do this all the time. No one usually gets stranded besides the tourists. But, um,"—he glanced around, smiling and nodding at certain people—"these are my friends, my family. We try to take care of each other as best we can."

Holly released a sob, and Cal pulled her into a warm hug.

"We're not perfect. We care, in our own ways."

Her voice quivered. "Even June and Suzanne?"

Cal chucked. "Especially June and Suzanne." He stroked her hair, studying her curled form. There was more to this woman than he knew. She was obviously smart and hard working, but here she was writing up candy store reviews. What had happened for her to end up here?

"I don't think the world has been treating you right, Holly." He rocked her back and forth, and she reveled in the gesture's comfort. "You should hang around with us some more and see what caring neighbors look like."

“I don’t….” She didn’t know what to say. Her family had always been cold and indifferent. They were so task-driven that they tolerated nothing but perfection. They were big successes, and she wanted to be one as well. Did she want to be out in dangerous situations with her life in danger to please some goal her parents assigned her?

She gazed into Cal’s blue eyes, and a wave of emotions rode over her. A night of nookie in the tent was the tip of the iceberg. That look said she and Cal were more than a one-night stand, more than a shared snack of strawberry jelly beans, more than cooking candy in a cozy kitchen.

It spelled out a life Holly would enjoy.

Cal made a good point about being in a war zone. How would she ever cope with live-fire if a sudden storm scared the bejesus out of her. She enjoyed writing about dog shows, school talent nights, and local beauty pageants. Okay, not the pageants, but she didn’t mind the minor events, the ones important to a few special people. All she needed was a chilly night on a mountain, in the arms of a warm man to show her.

"I have to work, Cal." She attempted to be her usual prickly self, but he didn't buy it.

"I know a guy with a candy shop. He might need an assistant…" He rocked her again, and she suppressed a bubbling giggle. He obviously wanted her to stay, but her working in a shop seemed far below her potential. And too much time together spelled trouble.

"Oh, please," she countered. "You have enough staff."

He pressed his head on top of hers. "You may be right. There's another guy with a B&B who needs a cook…."

"Cal." Remorse filled her words, and tears threatened again. "I can't just…"

"Okay, here's what we do." Mr. Fix-It to the rescue. "You ask your boss to file the story electronically, take a week off from work. I'll work out a deal with Russ to give you room and board for the week. You hang out here and see if you like it. We could go on an actual date and everything."

She pulled away from him, searching his gaze. "And if I don't like it here?" Her words drowned in fear and sorrow, and Cal blinked at her as if he held back tears.

"Then…" The word sounded strangled, and he cleared his throat. "Then me and my broken heart will wish you the best." He kissed the top of her head. "I don't do pressure, Holly. I want you to stay, or at least date me from your town, your state, or whatever. I want you to be happy, and I'm betting Bakersville will be a great place for you. It's your choice."

She blinked at him, and the decision was easy. She'd stay the week. It'd take time to find a new job, a new place. They would feel their way. One thing was for sure: letting go of Cal was not an option, not now, not ever.

He was a keeper.

Chapter Fifteen

Back at the B&B, freshly showered and fed, Cal curled beside Holly as she slept. She held tight to his arm, which wrapped around her under the covers. She'd had a few hits in the past twenty-four hours. The storm, their escapade in the tent, the town coming for them. What happened in her past to cause the storm to be so overwhelming?

He wanted to know everything. To spend every day finding out more about this brave and vulnerable woman. He hoped she'd want to try. She appeared to like his idea of a vacation in Bakersville for a week. They'd have a chance to really talk, not try to push through their time together like a checklist.

His own eyelids sagged with sleep. He had a huge pile of things to do today, but they needed sleep in a warm bed first and maybe…

Holly rolled over, her grip shifting slightly to adjust her movement. Sleepy and warm, she kissed him, and Cal threw his own checklist out the window. It could wait.

Every bit of it.

He woke as the bed shifted. Holly rose, dropped her sheet, and walked naked to the secret bathroom. He smiled, enjoying the sight of her beautiful backside swaying in the afternoon light. She closed the door, and he felt bereft. They were at the beginning, too soon for an open bathroom door or even morning breath.

He checked his own breath. The hotel must have an extra toothbrush somewhere. If not, toothpaste on his finger worked just fine for morning (midafternoon?) breath.

They showered, and even though he wore Ladies Delicate Rose deodorant, he didn't stink. He flopped on his back, staring at the lacy canopy overhead. Not Russ's style, but it kind of sold the place. B&Bs appealed to the frou-frou tourists. Russ could do the place as a large Airbnb. Then he wouldn't have to cook.

The door opened as Cal's stomach grumbled loudly. Holly stood in the doorway with a T-shirt covering her lovely curves. "Hungry?" she asked with a quirk of her eyebrow.

"For food? Yes."

She rolled her eyes at his response. "Diner or pizza?"

"Yes," Cal said with a grin.

She exited the bathroom and tossed his shirt at him, hitting him right in the face. "Get moving, mister."

Once changed and dressed, they headed out the door to the diner. They didn't spot Russ on their way in or out of the Inn. Perhaps he went out to interview someone or to hire a cleaner. Cal hoped Russ spoke to Wendy about the chef's job and took her to dinner to celebrate.

"Hey, I gotta make a quick stop at the store. I've been MIA too long. Can I meet you at the diner?"

Holly glanced at her phone. "Sure. I want to check something with Russ." She dashed inside the inn. A stray idea tickled his brain, and he let it pass. Russ was a handsome dude, but Holly never looked at the man twice.

He headed down the block to the store, dreading the absence, but life happened. He never let a day pass without making or prepping something. The life of a small business owner dictated constant, tiny tasks to do every single day. He needed to check on the beans he and Holly had started, prep the caramels, and check the nut supply in the storeroom.

He sighed.

So much happened in such a short time. She had interviewed him, but so much had happened. Cal needed time to process. His wild mind needed a long run or a few hours in the kitchen doing monotonous tasks to work through his emotions. But not until after a meal at the diner.

Holly was probably asking Russ about staying longer at the inn. Well, Cal hoped so. Ninety percent of him wanted to follow Holly, but duty called. Besides, he felt sure Russ would accommodate the extra time. Then,

Wendy could do a trial run breakfast for him to audition for the cook position.

Cal banged through the front door, his mind still on the B&B and Wendy. He hoped it didn't appear if he wanted to fire her. The Inn might be a great opportunity for her and…

He stopped short a few feet into the store. Suzanne stood blocking the door to the kitchen, her arms crossed. Of course, her expression and body language didn't register immediately. When Cal got lost in his own head, he missed all sorts of cues.

"Hey, Suzanne. Sorry it took me so long to get here today. I'll get started." He brushed past her, his mind on the small batch of jelly beans from the other day. They were probably a bust. Such a shame because they were the first thing he and Holly created together.

In the kitchen, he pulled the trays and placed them on the counter. The sound of a clearing throat sank into his mind, and he popped his head up to find Suzanne in the room. He narrowed his gaze, and her tense posture clicked. He was in trouble.

Again.

"I'm just…"

"What the hell, Cal?" she barked. Her brow furrowed, and her mouth formed a scowl. She glared at him, waiting for an answer.

Ten ideas ran through Cal's mind. The hike? Holly? The storm? The night with Holly? The morning with Holly? Trusting June with the hike? Pushing Wendy toward Russ? The last one must be it. He'd said nothing about Wendy's new job. Suzanne managed the store. He should have told her.

"I'm sorry." His hands fell from the counter. "I should've asked you about it. I got wrapped up in the moment..."

Suzanne stepped back and clutched at her collar. "Cal? What are you saying? Asking me? My God, why would you think that?"

He shrugged and paced toward the baker's rack. He pulled out several sheets, considering making a large batch of old-fashioned mints for Russ, and put his mind in automatic mode.

"She's perfect for the job. We both know it, and you and I can pick up the slack. Or even hire someone else. We'll be fine for a few weeks until the wrinkles smooth out."

Suzanne staggered. "What are you talking about?" She blinked at him, a helpless expression in her eyes.

Cal stared at the woman wide-eyed. Maybe she wasn't mad at him about Wendy. "What are *you* talking about?"

She huffed and marched over to the counter, leaving the clean surface between them. "I'm talking about the reporter. What are you talking about?" She growled at Cal, adding to his confusion.

He scratched his head. "Wendy. I told Russ to call Wendy and maybe hire her on as a cook. I never got the chance to ask her about it. I figured with her skills at decorating the candy, she'd be a wonderful cook too."

"Wendy!" Suzanne threw her hands into the air.

"Yeah." He stepped back, unsure where her pure rage spawned from.

She slammed her hands on the counter. "You told Wendy to find another job?" She snorted. "Probably a good idea after all the damage you've done to our store."

Heat crept up his neck. "Excuse me?" He kept his tone inquisitive, but the heat of anger boiled under his skin.

"You're careless, Cal. I warned you, but you never listen." She paced back and forth in front of the counter. "I told you the reporter would be trouble. But you went right ahead and danced her all around town. Wined and dined her." She glared at Cal. "And you dragged her up the mountain."

Suzanne's words slowly sank into his head. He worked to shove aside all thoughts of Wendy and focus on her anger over Holly. Why was she so upset? What did she warn him about?

"Hold on," he started. He held up his hands to stop her from moving and allow him to focus. "You're mad about the hiking trip?"

Suzanne spun to face him, her hand slapping the counter again. "I'm furious you slept with her!"

Cal danced back until his butt hit the door. *What the hell?* He blinked at Suzanne, hurt and irritated for such a statement to come from her mouth. He shook his head to clear it. She was his employee, not his grandmother.

"First, how did you know? Second, my personal life is none of your business." He crossed his arms, but felt like a small child trapped in the corner.

Suzanne flapped her arms again. "First,"—she delivered the words with a sneer—"everyone knows. Second, when you can't keep it in your pants with someone who could make or break our store…"

Bricks of emotions fell into place as Cal stared at his manager. Suzanne ran a good show. She managed the store, managed him dealing with his ADHD, and usually she kept the bossing and bullying to a minimum.

But she crossed the line.

He owned the store, he made the candies, and he was a grown man. Deftly, he stepped around the counter but kept a few feet between them. He gazed at her, trying to keep his expression calm and neutral but not friendly.

"Suzanne," he said, and almost fist-pumped at how cool his tone sounded. "I'm the owner of the shop." He met her gaze with one eyebrow raised. The gesture alone appeared to cow her a bit.

He continued, "My relationship with Holly is not your business. If you have questions about it, I'm delighted to answer them. I will not"—he took a small step toward her—"let you chastise me about it or its impact on my store." He emphasized the word "my" a little.

Suzanne retreated toward the shop door but still threw out, "And what about Wendy?"

He rolled his eyes, blocking her deflection. "You do a great job managing the store, but you are not *my* manager. I understand you were nervous about what Holly might write about us. I assure you she's a consummate professional. No matter what happens between us, she will deliver a truthful article about my store."

She stepped backward again, closer to the shop door. "But you compromised yourself and the store on that mountain. And I find out afterward that you fired Wendy. Really, Cal. I can't…"

He sighed and moved to stand beside her, not to intimidate but to reassure. He placed a hand on her shoulder. "I put too much on your plate, Suzanne. I'm not sure why you are so violently upset. I also don't know why you think it's okay to talk to me like I'm your employee or your son. I'm not." He squeezed her shoulder. "Wendy is not fired. She's not full-time and could use more income. Russ might provide that."

Suzanne stuttered and stammered. "Oh, not fired? I didn't know. I never meant…"

Cal pulled her into him for a full-body hug. "I know you didn't, but I think a vacation is in order. Take a day or two, even a week off. Decide if you still want to manage the store or try something new."

A sob burst from her lips. "Please don't fire me. I'm sorry. I didn't mean to be harsh."

Cal rocked her gently. "I know. You've been so angry for a long time, Suzanne. You need some healing. Your job is safe here, as long as you never talk to me that way again."

He pulled her back to meet her gaze. She smiled at him with a watery expression.

"Deal."

Holly practically skipped, walking hand in hand to the diner with Cal. This all might work in the end. She just had some serious life planning to do. She and Cal rounded the corner and headed inside the diner. The usual crowd filled the booths. The person in the last booth forced Cal to stop in his tracks. A white-haired woman sat serenely, her hands folded on the table. She met Holly's gaze, and a little smile crossed her lips.

Cal let go of Holly's hand and beelined for the booth. "Hey, Grandma."

Holly stopped mid-stride. *His grandmother? Oh crap.* She planned to interview the woman today for a fuller history of the shop. Plus, she was his sole living relative, and Cal and Holly just… Her stomach squished with the thought of "meeting his family." She pulled in a huge breath and followed him to the last booth.

Cal kissed the older woman on the cheek and turned to Holly with a grin. "Holly Lincoln, please meet my grandmother, Beatrice McIntyre, Bea. Grandma, meet Holly, the reporter doing the story on the shop."

The woman, the perfect model of a small-town old lady, pursed her lips. "Seems as if she's more than a reporter. Cal, don't blow smoke up my…" She folded her hands, her mouth twitching.

"Well, uh…" He glanced at Holly, then his grandma, and back to Holly. He held out a hand for her to sit.

She slid over, keeping enough room for him beside her. Awkwardness filled the space between them.

"Let's get you some food," Bea said, her voice tight. She raised her hand, and Tess walked over with three plates.

She'd ordered for them. *Interesting.*

Holly stared at the food, suddenly not hungry. In the past, when she'd met the boyfriend's family, her stress level shot into the stratosphere. What if his family acted like hers? The two had just met, fallen for each other, and now she had to meet the woman who raised him. Granted, they'd planned the talk all along, his grandmother being the original owner of the candy shop, but still…

Holly blinked as the epiphany hit. In her head, she'd called Cal her boyfriend. A small smile crossed her lips.

She gazed at her plate, hoping she'd eat enough to satisfy the woman. She glanced over at Cal, who tucked in with relish. Her smile grew wider. Who at the diner wanted Cal's help? He'd already had his own rescue today.

"So, what were you thinking hiking on the mountain, young man?" His grandmother's voice sounded soft and not accusatory, more questioning in a passive-aggressive way.

Cal swallowed hard. "June thought it'd be fine. She wouldn't have taken us up…"

His grandmother pointed a finger at him. "June didn't check the weather accurately, did she?" she asked tightly. The menace in her voice seemed to rise.

"June doesn't have your trick knee, Grandma. Thanks for lunch, by the way." He shoveled another mouthful into his gullet.

Holly shook her head and took a dainty bite of her blue plate special—meatloaf, mashed potatoes, and a scoop of boiled veggies. The meatloaf didn't taste half-bad and reminded her of her own grandmother's favorite standard meal. She put her fork down, sensing the rise in tension.

"What June doesn't know is going to kill her. Look at her ankle." Bea pointed a fork at Cal. "Walking around on a mountain with a cast. She's the one who should have spent the night in the cold and rain. Not my boy."

The woman appeared to be protective. Not good for Holly. If she knew what the two of them did on the mountain and at the inn, Holly would never be in the woman's good graces.

"Grandma..." His voice held the tiniest note of a whine. Cal turned away from the older woman, his fork poised to enter his mouth again.

Stress-eat much, my friend?

Holly covered her smile with her napkin. Not a good idea to get between a boy and his grandmother. Too bad Cal was a grown man.

"Now, Holly." Bea's sharpness and anger disappeared like smoke. The two met each other's gazes, and Holly felt a connection between them. Bea appeared to be solid, intelligent, and loving. But similar to the other women in town, like Suzanne or June, she hid it behind a façade of authoritarianism.

"I hope we will still receive a nice write-up even though this one"—she flicked a finger at Cal—"dragged you on a crazy adventure. I do not know what was in his head." She sighed, her lunch untouched. "All he needed to do was show you the shop, make fabulous candy, and introduce me. Instead, he..."

Holly held up a hand to cut her off. "I plan to write a nice piece on the shop, and if my editor lets me, I'll do a further follow-up on the town. The different shops, people, and how they came together to help us out." She smiled, but Bea frowned.

"Wait. Other shops?" She speared a carrot with her fork and wielded the vegetable at Holly. "You can't write about the other shops. The story was supposed to focus on my candy shop, my grandson featured, and our store getting lots of new business."

Holly sputtered. Had her boss made a deal with the woman? "Mrs. McIntyre, I planned to come to Bakersville to write a three-part article about Cal's shop." She emphasized his name, hoping the woman might understand her point. "There aren't any restrictions about what I include in the text." Holly crossed her arms.

The "meeting the family" thing had taken a bad turn.

Both women turned to Cal, who licked his lips and put down his fork. *Oh, good.* He'd put a fine point on it, and Holly wouldn't have to argue with the woman.

Tess stopped at their table, coffee pot in hand. "Cal, can you fix the sink? It's all stopped up, and Mel is cooking. She doesn't want to get filthy if she's cooking."

He grinned. "I'll be right back." He disappeared in a flash, Holly staring daggers at his retreating form.

She'd never seen him run from anyone else in town. He stood his ground with everyone, helping out or being a funny guy. Maybe, in the end, he was a coward. Her hopes fell. Was their crazy whirlwind nothing more than a tempest in a teapot?

Whatever that idiom meant.

Holly turned to Bea and said, "Say what you need to say. He's gone." She didn't want to dick around. If the woman intended to dislike her, so be it.

Bea sat against the booth with a smile creeping over her lips. "Direct. I like it because Cal…well, he's Cal."

"Circles," Holly said with no disparity. She appreciated how Cal wound himself through a conversation. It illustrated how his brain worked. She loved that his mind never thought in a single straight line. After years with newsies, someone who was *not* direct felt amazing.

"He told you about the allergy?" Bea lifted her chin, giving the simple sentence weight.

Holly's brow furrowed. "Yeah, no chocolate. He reacted badly as a kid, and you stopped including the item in your shop. Revamped the whole place, he said."

Bea lowered her chin. "You understand why. It's still a scar, but it's necessary. I don't want you or anyone else to push him into making a terrible choice."

The confusion of the conversation thickened. Holly studied Bea's expression. Her reporter's instincts said she'd missed something here.

"I'd never ask Cal to change. He's got a great product line. It's interesting, unique, and marketable. I'd encourage him to have an online presence but never ask him to sell chocolate."

Bea wagged a finger at her. "If you two are what I think you are, you can't have it either. I'm not losing him. He's all I have left."

Holly allowed the idea of no chocolate to flutter in her brain again for a second. She could give him that. She'd have to travel for work, anyway. Have her choco when she planned to be away from town for a while.

No cross-contamination.

No problem.

Wow, that was easy.

She pressed her lips and studied the floor. Too easy. She must like the guy. Like *really* like him.

She swallowed hard.

"He probably won't tell you, but I will because I see how you two look at each other. I'm not fool enough to believe you were saints in that tent while stuck on the mountain. You might leave tomorrow and never return. But I don't think it's the case." She folded her hands on the table, her expression resigned.

Holly held up a hand. She had an eerie feeling Bea was about to expose something about Cal. Something deeply emotional and tragic. His grandmother should not be the person to tell her Cal's most secret emotions or memories.

"I'm going to stop you right there, Bea. Cal and I are at the beginning of whatever this is. He hasn't told me all his life secrets and I haven't shared mine. We will get there. Rest assured that I would not ever spill someone else's personal tragedies in my articles."

Bea rolled her eyes, but Holly plowed on. "That's not what I write and not what I'm about. Even if he and I weren't involved, I wouldn't share things that don't need to be in the public know."

Bea sat back, her face a angry mask. Holly worked hard not to gulp. A nervous tingle ran from her stomach up her spine and out her limbs. She couldn't believe she just spoke to Cal's grand that way. The woman looked like she was about to blast Holly into next week.

"I see." Bea's words dropped like stone.

Holly glanced around hoping Cal would rush in and rescue her. His words rang true once again. *"What are you going to do in a war zone?"*

Phoebe's words repeated in her head. *"You're fucking good, and they have you writing about puppies."*

She didn't need anyone to save her. She was Holly Lincoln, ace reporter. Straightening her shoulders, she met Bea's gaze. "As far as the article is concerned, my intention is to highlight the success of your business. How you and he created a successful store in Bakersville. Not pull the sympathy card and make either of you appear pathetic. That's not what I do."

Speech over, she blotted her lips with her napkin, though she hadn't eaten a bite.

Bea narrowed her eyes, then grinned. Holly understood where Cal got his energy from. "Good," Bea said simply. "We will be able to work together after all."

Cal skidded to a halt in front of the table. "Sorry!" he gushed. "The sink… phew. We called Mario." He clapped his hands and rubbed them together. "What did I miss?"

Bea and Holly exchange another meaningful look. "Nothing, sugar," Bea said and waved at his seat. "Let's eat."

Chapter Sixteen

Holly raised a finger as Cal sat down. "I need to make a phone call."

Her head spun with all the information, activities, and events, but one thing remained at the center—Cal.

She'd completely fallen for the man. He was right about the war correspondent thing. In her heart, she didn't want that life. Her parents wanted her to succeed. In the end, Holly had to do what was best for her. If a big rainstorm reduced her to a quivering ball of jelly, what would the caves of Afghanistan or the streets of Gaza do to her?

She was good at her job, a talented writer, and an efficient reporter. She enjoyed some of the puff pieces. Not forever. But Cal was right. Plattsburg, Burlington, and even Albany weren't that far away. They'd be two hours from each other. Easily doable.

She ducked out of the diner and pulled out her cell. Milton answered on the first ring.

"Tell me the good news, Holly."

She grinned. "I have a good story here, several actually. I want to do more here in Bakersville."

Her editor chuckled. "Something about the candy maker, eh?"

"That obvious, huh? Also, there's much more in the North we don't cover. Summer's coming. The entire area has tons of activities, festivals, and fun. I could spend six months or more here writing everything."

The other end of the line went silent, and Holly checked her phone to see if the call had dropped.

"Milton?"

"Holly," he responded, his voice quiet. "Is that what you want? A few days ago…"

She sighed. "I know, but I learned things about myself over the past few days. I'm a talented reporter, but I'm no CNN correspondent. I want to work my way into TV news, most likely local."

"Not much excitement there."

She laughed. "Milton, I spent the night trapped on a mountain after a rain squall and a flash flood. No excitement?" She blew a raspberry into the phone.

"You what?"

Got him.

"I can write it as another story, but I outlined about five for Bakersville. Give me a chance to write about the area for a while, and I promise I will provide great articles for our readers."

Milton paused again. "So, I'm assuming you were stranded with the candy man and plan to move in with him tomorrow."

She frowned. "I'm playing my options after said candy man saved my life." Yeah, not exactly the truth, but a few grains of it. Only a man like Cal could say those truths and have her listen. He asked her what she wanted, and she discovered she wanted him.

Only him.

"So, I want more trips here. And if you can't accommodate, I'm going to try some local papers and news agencies. I could find a home here."

"You got it, Holly. Send me the article, and we will talk follow-ups."

She ended the call and dashed into the diner, hope filling her heart.

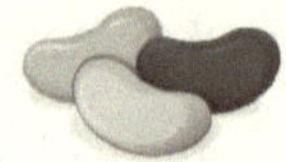

Cal grabbed a fork and dug into his food. Across the table, Grandma cleared her throat. Immediately, he put the utensil on his plate and focused his attention on her.

She smiled, placing her napkin on the table. "While we wait for Holly,"—her gaze pinned him to the seat—"we can talk about this business between you and her."

He leaned back, anger spiking in his blood. Suzanne all over again. "Grandma, what's between me and Holly is between me and Holly." He crossed his arms, done with the conversation.

Grandma mirrored his pose. "I'm aware. I worry about you."

He leaned forward, his finger pointing at the woman, ready to blast her. The temptation to rage about everyone telling him what to do sparked in his chest. He and Holly had much to work out, and it was no one else's business.

They had a lifetime to figure out if they liked each other enough to stay together. Not the first time he'd fallen for someone in a few days, but man, he hoped it was the last. He didn't need the other women in his life to bury him with advice.

He recalled how the conversation with Suzanne ended. He put a hand out toward his grandmother, the woman who raised him, who loved him unconditionally. She placed her hand in his.

"Gram, I'm good. We're gonna talk. We're gonna figure it out. I promise you, Holly will not trash the store to get back at me. The woman is the pillar of integrity." He chuckled. "If she can ignore Russ's kitchen fire, then she can be cool if we don't work out."

She squeezed his hand. "And you're sure?"

Cal grinned, a warm feeling blanketing his body. "Yes. I'm one hundred percent positive."

They smiled at each other and waited for Holly to return.

Holly interviewed Bea while they ate their lunch. She avoided asking about Cal's parents or his allergy. The woman knew a wealth of fun facts and cute stories about Cal, most of which would be useless for the article.

Once they completed the meal with no more emergencies for Cal, the three left the diner. Bea waved and headed down the street while Cal and Holly stood on the diner's step. She pulled the yellow scarf from her pocket, a gift from the rescue team. She wrapped it around her neck without a thought.

Nervousness mixed with a sense of belonging rolled through Holly's body. Bakersville was growing on her in a bright, sunny fashion. And Cal… All her emotions for him felt like a mushed-up ball of yarn. Red yarn, like his hair.

A small smile passed her lips as she glanced at her shoes. Who knew where they'd end up, but a plan could only help. She pulled in a deep breath, ready for their next conversation. She wanted him to initiate the talk, afraid she'd blurt out thoughts she meant to hold on to for a bit. She had big feelings for the man, but that info could wait a few weeks or months.

The yellow scarf scratched her neck, and she yanked it off. Not yet. She needed more time before she could wear yellow without feeling exposed.

"So, uh…" Cal gazed at the sky, scratching the back of his neck. "You still leaving today?" His words sounded tremulous and sweet.

Holly's smile escaped again. She glanced at him without lifting her head. "About that…"

Cal huffed, crossing his arms, not an angry gesture but a disappointed one.

She stifled a laugh. "My boss is cool, and I checked with Russ. I'll stay another night or two and write the article. And…"

She turned to him. He stared at the sky with arms crossed. She grazed her fingers over his chin, turning his face to hers. "And we can talk and figure it out."

Cal exploded. Well, not exactly exploded, but in one swift motion, he pulled her into his arms, his lips on hers.

She allowed the passionate kiss that curled her toes to linger for a moment before pushing away.

"We've got a lot to figure out."

He refused to allow her to move more than an inch. "We do," he breathed and rubbed his hands down her back to her hips. "Any ideas about…" They gazed at each other, and they both knew they wanted it, needed it. They'd found the right person at the wrong time.

Holly brushed her lips over his, reminiscent of the first kiss in the kitchen. "I like you, Cal. We'd have to be long distance for a bit. Until I find a way to make it work."

"I know," he said. The hungry look faded from his eyes. "We just met. I'd never ask you to move to Bakersville on the chance you and I might work. I want to find out if we will, though. You seem to understand me. No one ever does. I don't want to miss out on something great because of my shop. I…"

Holly gasped and put a finger over his lips. No way on God's green Earth she'd allow him to give up the shop or even move it. He was perfect, right here, in his town, with its odd people and deep friendships. Holly could move and be flexible, but she needed more time to see where their relationship went.

"No talk about the store. The store is an immovable object we will work around. Even if Suzanne can run things for you."

Cal laughed and pulled back. "I forgot to tell you about the conversation she and I had. She got bossy, and I reminded her that she was the manager, not the owner. I make the decisions, call the shots. Not her. She was mad, but in the end, she realized how much she overstepped."

Holly bounced on her toes, glad to hear Cal also knew who owned the store. She'd worried he just let the woman run the show. "I'm glad you stood up to her. I hate the way she seems to cut you down all the time, as if she's the boss. Good for you."

"Is there a chance?" he asked, his eyes full of hope.

"A chance I will be dropping by Bakersville often in my reporter travels? Yes. I spoke to my editor about covering the area full-time. I'll be living downstate, though. I'm not ready to move."

It was Cal's turn to bounce. "It's way too early for us to even consider, but you'd always have a place to stay."

Holly bit her lip. "Yeah, that's what Russ said." She pulled away with a giggle, moving out of his reach.

"Hey," he mock-growled. "Russ can find his own reporter. You're mine."

Holly slid forward again into his embrace. "Am I?"

"Well," Cal said, his head cocked to the side. "Only if you like jelly beans."

"I'm on it."

The End

Also by Ginny Frost

The Oakwood Tavern Series

The Bar Scene, Oakwood Tavern 1

Terese Brock manages the Oakwood Tavern with style and grace. Unfortunately, she's trying to avoid her employer's IRS disaster and her own debts. She needs a new job—fast. Terese hopes to land an executive position at the new conference center, the perfect solution to all her money woes.

For months, Drew Drake has admired Terese from afar, but she doesn't know he exists. He's thrilled when his humor and persistence catch her eye. And when she takes him home, he discovers she's everything he expected, and so much more.

Drew fails to mention he's the heir to one of the most successful businesses in town, the force behind the new conference center. Rather than clue her in, he decides to let her get to know the real him. When she walks into her interview, ready to kick ass and take names, her universe shatters.

Behind the desk sits her boy-toy, Drew.

Swindled, Oakwood Tavern 2

For years, Marley Volkov's survival depended on conning people out of their life savings. One look into Alan Reid's pained eyes, with his soiled reputation and heap of financial problems, awakens a new empathy inside her. She renounces grifting forever and not just because every inch of her burns to be with him. But his association with her and her checkered past will drag him further into the gutter. To save herself, to save him, she must walk away. Walk away from the unbridled desire he inspires, from the passion and sympathy that feel like home.

Alan Reid is buried to the neck in money issues. The understanding and compassion he finds in Marley is the exact thing he needs at the completely wrong time. Everything about her makes his blood run hot. She's smart, irresistible, and a criminal. Why is the only person who's ever shown him sympathy have to be a con artist? He can't be with her, but he's compelled to save her from herself.

Stranded, Oakwood Tavern 3

Where the hell is Conrad?

While his business partners back at The Oakwood Tavern think he's on the run for tax evasion, for Conrad Bennett, it's a whole other story. One that includes being stranded on an island in the South Pacific with no cell phone, no money, and no passport.

Good thing he just slept with the only woman on the island with a plane.

Vivian Costa has her own problems. She's on this remote island for a much needed, much overdue, self-imposed exile. But now her one-night stand wants not only a ride off the island, but to find out who has set him up. So much for laying low and hiding out. Vivian knows she should walk away, but there's something about Conrad that won't let her.

It's time to figure out how to rescue each other.

When Hearts Collide, Oakwood Tavern 4, Sandy Bay 5

Planning and organizing the wedding this weekend left Stacey Montgomery little time for fun. She's woefully behind on her Bucket List from the bridal shower. Right now, on the plane to Massachusetts, it's her last chance to cross off number three. Luckily, there's a hottie sitting next to her, and he looks promising. And if her plan succeeds, she might invite him for all the other winter activities on the list.

After working through a criminal IRS audit at his job in Iverton, Eric Holmes could use some rest and relaxation. Usually, bad luck plows him flat like a steamroller, but this time his friend Pete caught the bad juju. With his bestie in a cast from a skiing accident, Eric gladly took Pete's place to tend bar at a destination wedding on the Atlantic coast. Then, he sat next to the most beautiful woman—blonde, curvy, and…

She just asked him to join the mile-high club

Gulp.

But how can he say no?

Stonewater Stories

The Carriage House, Stonewater Stories Book 0.5

Homeless, jobless, and newly single, Cheryl Winston-Bristol finds herself back at her oppressive childhood home. Even at the Carriage House of their estate, she can't escape her overbearing mother and tyrant of a grandfather from making her life miserable. That is until she discovers her high school crush, Ted Kramer, repairing the steps. The dozen years of handyman repairs have molded him into quite a hunk.

Ted working around her house every day? Yes, thank you.

Desperate for the work, Ted Kramer of Kramer and Sons agreed to take the job at the Winston-Bristol's Carriage House. Ted is both excited and terrified since most of their family hates his. Then he discovers Cheryl is home and living in the Carriage House. Working in the same place with the beautiful, classy Cheryl terrifies and excites him. He can handle seeing the charming Cheryl all summer, can't he?

In this prequel to the Stonewater Stories, learn how Ted and Cheryl found each other. To hear their happily ever after, read all of the Stonewater Stories.

Christmas Sparks, Stonewater Stories Book 1

Kindergarten teacher, Margaret Porter, is looking forward to the best Christmas holiday in years. Without her irresponsible ex-husband causing chaos, she and her two children can finally have a fun, peaceful celebration. Everything looks picture perfect until her living room catches fire.

Volunteer firefighter, Ryan Kramer, never knew what hit him when he rescues a reluctant and quick-tempered Margaret from her burning home. But it's more than sympathy for her situation that gets under his skin. Her sassy, no-nonsense attitude bowls him over.

Margaret finds her family rescued by Ryan again and again. Something about him speaks to her soul, and she discovers it hard to resist him. Unlike her careless and manipulative ex-husband, Ryan's nothing but wonderful throughout the entire ordeal.

As Ryan investigates the damage to Margaret's home, he discovers his family's business, Kramer and Sons, worked on the fire-ravaged room. Did shoddy work by his family put a single mom and her two kids out in the cold at Christmas? Can Margaret see beyond his last name and fall for him too?

Christmas Affair, Stonewater Stories Book 2

Josephine Lockwood spent her entire life in a sickbed being coddled by her anxious mother. Finally, after receiving the correct diagnosis for her illness, she's standing on the edge of a new adventure. She's finished her audition program for an online gaming platform and is poised to move out of her family home. But she must attend her mother's annual Christmas party.

Brett Kramer, a hard-working handyman, is finishing up renovations at the Excelsior Hotel in Iverton when Jo drops into his life. She's cute, friendly, and totally intriguing. Too bad he's at work. The family contracting business is suffering thanks to a bogus complaint, and he doesn't want any whiff of impropriety to taint the current contract.

But when Jo flees from her mother's party, Brett steps in to help her escape, disregarding his business's reputation.

Their departure only complicates the situation. A snowstorm, sibling rivalry, and an overprotective mother forces them together and tears them apart. Jo and Brett must find a balance to make their relationship more than a Christmas Affair.

Christmas Baby, Stonewater Stories Book 3

He'd heard the rumors she was back in town. He had to see for himself.

As Ted Kramer steeled himself to knock on the hotel room door, the last thing he was prepared to see was the woman who shattered him holding a baby. Cheryl Winston-Bristol had been the love of his life. And when she abruptly left town last year after their secret summer romance, it destroyed him. He couldn't eat. Couldn't sleep. Couldn't work. Yet here she is, baby and all. His baby. Merry Christmas to him.

When Cheryl realized she was pregnant, she knew her controlling and manipulative grandfather would never accept a Kramer child into his family. The feud between the Kramers and Winston-Bristols had dragged on for forty years and as long as that cantankerous man was alive, it would continue raging. Except now he's dead, and Cheryl has taken the opportunity to return to Stonewater for the

services. She knows she needs to tell her mother-- and Ted-- about the baby, but she never wanted him to find out about his daughter like this, though.
Maybe, just maybe, baby Harper will be the Christmas gift these families need to move on and find love again.

New Year's Miracle, Stonewater Stories Book 4

This past Christmas, Beverly Winston-Bristol's entire world has flipped on its side. Her beloved father passed away, and her errant daughter, Cheryl, has returned with a new baby, a Baby Kramer at that.
Beverly must heal old wounds for the sake of Baby Harper. If she continues her vendetta against David Kramer and his sons, she'll not only lose Cheryl again but her first grandchild as well. But being near David still hurts. Now that they are grandparents together, can Bev deal with having him back in her life?
On New Year's Eve, Harper's crib collapses. Alone with the baby, Beverly has no choice but to call David to rescue her.
Enjoy this sweet edition to the Stonewater Stories.

The Mortar & Pestle Series

Artist: A Second Chance Romance

Lexi Pintari is stuck in a dead-end cubicle job that is slowly killing her. She tucked away her passion for art when the love of her life ghosted her after college. Witnessing her lack of motivation, Lexi's best friend drags her to an art retreat for much-needed reflection and inspiration. Though knowing her ex-boyfriend is an artist-in-residence there, Lexi agrees to go. Unfortunately, her metal-goth style and enthusiasm for graphic comics clash with the pastel-scarf-wearing, tea-sipping participants, making her ex the least of her problems.
Cole MacDougall is blocked. His rise to the top of the modern art scene is crushed by a missing muse. He is desperate to paint again, but the canvas remains blank. Due to the shortage of patronage revenue, he is forced to put up with the groupie-students. Until he sees a woman standing out like a sore thumb in ripped jeans and a leather jacket. Lexi. Hope blooms that he can renew his passion through her.

About the Author

Ginny Frost is an indie author with four great series. She writes contemporary romance with a sexy, funny kick. In her downtime, she plays clerk at the local library—the perfect job to feed her reading addiction.

She lives in upstate NY with her very own kindhearted ogre, their two brilliant and creative children, and an evil cat named Flash.

www.ingramcontent.com/pod-product-compliance
Lightning Source LLC
LaVergne TN
LVHW091112080826
845145LV00008B/1883

* 9 7 8 1 9 6 5 8 9 9 2 1 2 *